REVELATION COUNTDOWN

REVELATION COUNTDOWN

SHORT FICTION BY CRIS MAZZA
IMAGES BY TED ORLAND

BLACK ICE
BOOKS

Published by Fiction Collective Two with support given by
the English Department Publications Unit of Illinois State
University, the English Department Publications Center of
the University of Colorado at Boulder, and the Illinois Arts
Council

Address all inquiries to: Fiction Collective Two, c/o English
Department, Publications Center, Campus Box 494, University of Colorado at Boulder, Boulder, CO 80309-0494

Revelation Countdown
Cris Mazza

ISBN: Paper, 0-932511-54-6, $7.00

Produced and printed in the United States of America
Distributed by The Talman Company

Cover image: Ted Orland
Book design: Jean C. Lee

Our thanks to Austin Peay State University and the Center for the Creative Arts at Austin Peay for their generous support at the inception of this project.

To Jim and Frances,
With love

Acknowledgements are made to the following publications in which these pieces first appeared:

High Plains Literary Review: "Guys With Trucks in Texas and California"

Fabric of Desire (Crossing Press): "Between Signs"

Yellow Silk: "On the Circuit"

Lovers (Crossing Press): "On the Circuit"

Confrontation: "Revelation Countdown"

Fiction International: "Three-Inch Tongue" and "Revelation Countdown" (Images by Ted Orland)

CONTENTS

GUYS WITH TRUCKS IN TEXAS AND CALIFORNIA

The way people treat animals shows you what kind of place it is. In California in the 19th century or early 20th, ranchers devised a round-the-campfire entertainment by chaining a bear to a tree and making it fight with a long-horned bull. That's California for you. Even a farmer in someplace like North Dakota wouldn't treat a dirty *pig* like that. Why'd they ever leave Connecticut to move *here*, and how'd her elegant brother manage to end up a dentist in Texas, both of them stuck in places where there're lots of guys who drive trucks, the kind of people who dump kittens on the side of the road.

On the hottest day of the year in San Diego, it was also a hot day in Texas (but it wasn't breaking any records). A guy chained an adult cougar in his pick-up truck, parked outside in direct sun. No one knows where the guy went, maybe those saloons with mechanical horses are still popular. Witnesses said the animal was leaping about desperately because the metal truckbed was like a hot griddle, then the cat jumped out of the truck and strangled itself on its chain. The owner, when notified, laughed and said, "Anyone need a rug?"

Meanwhile back in California, there's a new law in San Diego. You can't let a dog ride loose in the back of a pick-up truck. They can't quite justify making a law purely for an animal's sake, so they say it's a hazard to general safety when a dog bounces out of a truck on the freeway, hitting other cars and causing related havoc. So you have to tie the dog in the truck. The publicity campaign showed a dog with a shoulder harness and straps that fastened him to both sides of the truck. But the law just says the dog must be tied, so you know how they're going to tie them (if they even bother to do anything). People who have trucks are only going to have Dobermans or Doberman-mixes, Labs or Lab-mixes, German Shepherds or related mixes. Nothing small, nothing dainty, nothing cute, nothing with a high-pitched voice. If they aren't dog enough to ride loose in the back of a truck, what goddamn use are they? That's how you talk while riding in a truck. Have you ever seen a poodle in the back of a truck? If you wanted to have an attack-trained dog, wouldn't a poodle make a lot more sense? The surprise element. The dog'll be surprised all right, when it's bounced out of the truck and doesn't even have a fighting chance to land on its feet because the truck's still doing 65 or 70 and that beautiful black collar with silver studs breaks the dog's neck or drags it along the pavement, like the desperados did to the sheriff, behind their horses, in lawless Texas. But it's not a hazard for other motorists. When Glenda rode loose in the back yesterday, it was different because she was under a pile of tarps. Probably painter's tarps. That's what they smelled like. She was tied, but not *to* anything. He hasn't said where they're going and she hasn't asked, but she can see the signs that say east, and Texas is east of California. In Texas, her brother also has a truck. But that doesn't really count because he lives in a luxury apartment and grows herbs in a planter box and doesn't have a dog. She's been having a lot of time to think about stuff like this.

This is one of those trucks where the bumper is at eye level with other drivers—because the tires are so big. Huge tractor tires but the same economy truck body, and, of course, a black metallic roll bar behind the cab with shiny silver lights mounted on top. There's always going to be one parked at any all-night grocery—the guy's inside getting cigs and a burrito, his dog waiting in the back of the truck. But she waits inside the cab and he brings potato chips or a soda. She asked for cheese and an apple. That's what she craves. Everyone's going to notice how wrong she looks—she doesn't look like the girls who are sometimes with the guys whose trucks have big tires. They have long dirty-blond unsilky hair, the slightest hint of frizz, gum chewers, and if they wear any make-up it's just on their eyes and they never put it on very well, sometimes making a dark line of mascara under each eye so their eyes look upside-down. They follow the guy into an auto parts store or hardware store or the all-night grocery, and they scuff their feet because they're wearing plastic thongs or house slippers, and because it's almost always warm in Cali-

13

fornia they wear their tube-tops or spaghetti-strap blouses year-round. That's probably why he doesn't want her to get out of the truck since she put on low-heeled leather sandals before they left, and a satin mini shirt-dress with a picture of Beethoven which she bought for over $100 at a charity auction. Looks bad in a truck. But she told him—when he slowed up beside her, just as she was leaving her bank's automatic teller machine, and asked if she wanted a lift—she said, "I don't do trucks." He went around the block and slowed up again. Second time around is when she noticed his pit bull in the back of the truck, tongue to his knees, eyes glassy. She said, "Your dog needs a drink." He said "So do I," so he followed her home where first of all she filled a big bowl of water for the pit bull who slept in the shade on her condo's balcony while she was wrestled to the bed. But what about when the pit bull wakes up and is hungry or uses up the water? He could've just as easily taken the dog with them.

It's going to be okay as soon as they get to Texas because that's where her brother Olin is, filling teeth and adjusting braces, fitting dentures. He could've been a dentist *any*where, why Texas? This guy, what's'z'name, doesn't even know what kind of fuss is going to be kicked up when he shows up with her in Texas. If he had known, he might've chosen to go north to Canada or south to Mexico, both places where a truck with big tires is as obvious as a neon sign advertising "Please don't trust me," or "Please rob me." He probably thought Texas is safer for him, but he doesn't know about Olin. First time in her life she can be thankful that beautiful, genteel Olin moved to doltish Texas. Why should she bother to try an escape now when a much more satisfying rescue is imminent. Not that there'll be a struggle or fight or showdown—Olin won't degrade himself by messing with this guy. You don't fight with a coyote to get him to give up his toy, you just go take the toy, that's that, just open the truck door, pick her up like a precious doll and say, "Come on, Mouse, time to go home." Would that finally mean home to Connecticut? In California no one knows her as Mousey. Can you imagine a modeling agency taking on someone named Mouse? Why *Mouse*? She never asked him. Maybe for her mousey brown hair She changed that. Maybe because she was always so quiet. Just being polite. If he'd moved to California with them he might've had to start calling her Glenda, when it became obvious she was certainly no longer a mouse, but he hadn't lived at home since she was eight. Naturally she's had a lot of time to plan this long-overdue reunion with Olin since it seems like there's only cowboy music on the radio, and this guy hardly ever says anything. Olin might not talk much either, but at least he probably has a tape deck so she can listen to classical or light rock. He always liked James Taylor. She couldn't believe it when she saw James Taylor is *bald* now. And his songs seem boring. The hot wind coming in the truck's window vents made enough noise to drown out the radio until the station was too far away to be reached anymore. She hardly noticed the songs turning into static because there's something she

15

hasn't quite got figured out: How will Olin find her? What if the truck's at a stoplight and Olin's on the sidewalk, or if they're parked at a coffeeshop and Olin stopped there for a newspaper, he might just walk past and not notice her. She might say, "Olin," gently, as he passed, but he still might not notice—she doesn't belong in a truck like this so he wouldn't think to look. It won't be like she's expected, like when he drove his new truck to California for his wedding reception last year. He'd married a Texan, maybe it was *her* idea for him to get a truck. Then with her dripping, drawling accent, she said, "Oh, from what Olin mentioned, I didn't know you'd be so grown up, dear." You don't tell someone who's 22 and a professional model that they're *grown up*. Maybe you'd say sophisticated or stylish or mature or independent. That's what Olin could've called her, if they'd had a chance to be alone so she could make it all obvious. She almost had a chance to go with him to the drugstore one evening, but Dad decided to go. She was already standing beside the truck, waiting for Olin. Not an economy truck: his has tweed bucket seats and custom teak interior and he uses it to take his wind-surf board to the lake. She'd look more than all right in Olin's truck. They used to look like each other, almost like twins, at least their baby pictures did, but nobody mentioned it during the reception. She'd gotten a new haircut and style for the occasion, but how was Olin to know it was any different from what it had been. Know what he noticed? Her ankles. She was playing with the cat on the floor beside his chair where he was reading or watching television or talking to their dad. All of a sudden he grabs her ankle and tells her it's too fat and should be slender, like Suzy's. Glenda was a fashion model and what was *Suzy*—she doesn't even know what Suzy was. They never had that sister-to-sister talk Suzy thought would be so good for her when she finally told them the lost truck key was on the bottom of the aquarium at her condo. But Olin will have to notice, and know something's amiss, when he sees his chic little sister in a truck with this guy. The guy's been calling her by her name, but she doesn't know his. She hasn't inquired. After he asked for her name, he said, "Don't you want to know mine?" She didn't answer. A few minutes later she said, "I'll call you Duke or Butch or Rover or Spike." He thought that was funny enough for a smack in the mouth. But since then started calling her Glennie. Nobody's ever called her that before. People who tie your wrists together shouldn't call you *Glennie*.

After they spend twenty years convincing you it's romance at its highest form to lie under the stars with a man, and maybe you even put luminescent stars on your bedroom ceiling, you find out that you have to sleep on your stomach because your hands are tied, and you drool all over the tarps you're using as a bed because if you breathe through your nose you'll be asphyxiated by the paint smell. And how about when Olin finds out about this: in the middle of the night he groans as though still asleep, but climbs on and takes you from the rear. Maybe wolves do it that way, but wolves don't make such a mess. He gently cleaned her afterwards with a wash-n-dry.

There was no one for miles, so she screamed at him, "Last night you wouldn't let me wash my face and you've had wash-n-drys all the time?"

"I just got 'em," he said, "when you made such a stink about your goddamn face. Shit, I thought you'd *thank* me, not crawl all over my ass."

Why should she dignify that with an answer.

❖

Twenty miles since the last gas pump, thirty miles before the next one, all of a sudden he has something to say.

"How come you haven't once started bawling?"

"People don't *bawl*, they weep."

"What?"

"*Cows* bawl"

"What're you talking about? How come you never cry?"

What if she did, and *he* wanted to comfort her? Sometimes it's easier to ignore a question than answer it.

❖

There was this gas station man with oily hair and a face like a weasel, skinniest face she'd ever seen. He stared at her while putting gas in the truck. It was a huge truck stop, about ten lanes with pumps, six and eight-wheelers huffing and puffing, everything covered with a visible layer of grease or grime or black exhaust. She hadn't even known what's'z'name was leaning on the bumper beside her, until he coughed and said, "Think we can find any fresh air around here? I'll share it with ya." Since when do guys with trucks concern themselves with air? She couldn't think of anything to say, unless she'd suggested he use a wash-n-dry as an air filter over his nose and mouth. But the weasel-faced man was there to get his money. She asked where the restroom was. "Think you can foller this?" the man said, "through that yaller door there, to yer right, down a long hall, then to yer left," then with an elbow jabbed what's'z'name in the ribs, winked and chuckled, "wimmin folk, eh? Trust her not to git herself lost?"

If she was the type, she might've put a knee in his balls. Instead, hands on hips, faced him eye-to-eye, but his kept shifting away. "And I suppose you think I can't balance my own checkbook, buy my own insurance, or decide for myself who and who not to bring home for a drink—"

The weasel-faced man put his hands up in surrender, still laughing. He had horrible yellow-brown teeth and breath like something had died in his mouth. Maybe she wouldn't've even cared at all, except for how Suzy held Olin's arm like the edge of a life raft and told their mother she'd done such a good job raising a real feminist man. She wasn't finished telling the weasel off, had only paused for breath, but what's'z'name touched her shoulder and said, "S'okay, go on, I'll wait here."

She did get lost—had to ask someone else for directions because she'd forgotten what the weasel had said—and when she got back to the truck found a Tootsie-pop on her seat. He had one in his own mouth too, a bulge in his cheek like a squirrel saving nuts.

Probably from now on she'll think air's *supposed* to smell like a painter's tarp. And he held onto her all night like she was going to get up and go somewhere. Bottom of the truck is lined with ridges so she woke with that groggy stumpy feeling, you push your feet ahead of you on the way to the bathroom instead of lifting them. The bathroom: a rest stop and they only have cold water. He pulled the tarp off her face, her eyes still shut, he whispered, "God, you're pretty this morning." Laughing would've been such an effort. But there were plenty of times it would've been true if someone wanted to say so, instead of, at most, messing up her hair and calling her Mouse. *Morning, Mousey.* You know what a mouse is? Something they torture in labs. Well, you come out of a restroom at some barren rest stop, no one calls you mouse. He waited by the truck. Trusted her to walk all the way from the bathroom by herself. Can't even see the marks on her wrists anymore, where he used to tie her. If it's been so long, why aren't they in Texas yet? A truck meant for backroads *takes* the backroads. Her brother's honeymoon was to San Simeon, the Hearst Castle , never would've made it if she'd gone ahead and put the sugar in the gas tank.

Is the Southwest really a desolate wasteland dotted with reststops, overnight campgrounds and truckers' cafes? When he buys candy, she saves it until they can't find any radio stations at all. Maybe it's just that even a lovesick cowboy's out-of-tune yodeling is better than listening to each other breathe. He really doesn't say much. He had a pack of gum and offered a stick of it to her, but he used the gum to tap on her arm to get her attention. She took a stick, then he took a stick. In less than five minutes it was like chewing wood pulp. He took another stick. The pack of gum was sitting on the seat between them, so she took another stick too. Then there was only one stick left.

"Aren't you going to say anything?" she blurted.

"What can I possibly say?" Then he broke the last stick of gum in half and carefully, like building a house of cards, placed one half on her leg.

Just when you think they're obsolete, you come across one of those mini-zoos, a reptile show beside a restaurant in the middle of nowhere. She was chewing caramel, took the blob out of her mouth and offered it to a tortoise. The goo was hanging from her fingers toward the animal's mouth, but what's'z'name stuck his hand in the way so when she let go, the candy landed in his palm.

"It gums up their innards," he said.

"How about what it does to *us*?"

"At least we've got dentists."

Do guys with trucks actually go to the dentist?

They looked at all the lizards and snakes and horned toads. When the owner of the zoo asked for a buck each (you pay to get *out*) the guy said, "For twenty wouldja let them all go?" But at the same time, he was paying the two dollars.

Watching the sagebrush race past the window, she asked, "How often do you see a dentist?"

"Don't keep track, d'you?"

"Let's not discuss this stupid subject."

The modeling agency had said if she ever wanted to do television work, she would have to have her teeth capped. She was going to bring it up to Olin, next time she saw him. Why not call from the next reststop and tell him that's why she's coming to Texas. But how many days has it been since she brushed her teeth?

How long did he sit there silently planning this: With a smile on half his face only, one eye crinkled shut, he handed her a fistful of hard candy and said, "You can't let these rednecks get to you." Sucky candy is better than a chocolate bar because it lasts longer and gives her something to do—concentrate on not making any slurpy sounds.

"Who said anything's getting to me, least of all *you*."

"No, not me, c'mere!" He grabbed her arm and towed her up to the nearest pot-bellied local, and in a voice liquid yet nasal, sliding out of his mouth like a snake: "Hey there, mister, think you could find this here little lady someplace where wimmin-folk powder their noses?" He had his arm around her as though they were some kind of couple. But most likely he hadn't actually known how badly she did want a little make-up base

22

and perhaps some rouge powder.

They came out of the two restrooms at the same time. "You're funny," she said. "I mean you're crazy. Have you been on some sort of sugar-high?"

"I must be." He was grinning. They were both grinning.

No more potato chips and soda in the cab of the truck. Even though the best they could offer in the way of salad was a bowl of lettuce and a token slice of pale tomato. Guys with trucks look different here, wherever they are. Lots of cowboy hats, ostrich feathers as decals on the front, or old and battered with sweat marks. But even indoors, across from her in the booth, what's-'z'name wore his baseball cap with BUD written across the front. He does take it off when he sleeps. For the first time last night he fell asleep first. He actually has curly hair hiding under his hat all day, she's sure it would be light or golden brown if he washed it. Maybe they'll find a place to wash up today. Even if they just had a bowl of water and bar of soap, she could help him. Does he know how good it feels to put your head into the hands of a stylist, massaging your scalp with shampoo and strong fingers which never pull any hair or get any soap in your eyes? Sometimes she falls asleep with her head in the sink, something you'd never dream of doing in a dentist's chair. You know what she could've done last night while he was asleep—she could've gotten up, gotten his hat and thrown it away somewhere. Or ripped it up and mangled it so it looked like some wild animal thought it was alive and killed it. She hadn't thought about it before, but wild animals could walk right past them when they're asleep and they'd never know it. But animals might be afraid to come close, the way he thrashes and moans at night. He was grinding his teeth, so she very gently opened his mouth and made him stop. Just a very light "shhhh" and a feathery touch on his temple makes him sleep calmer too. Maybe he misses his dog. That's what's wrong. If she'd ever found out his name, she could ask him if he misses his dog, but you can't just blurt out, Do you miss your dog? It's got to be David, do you miss your dog? or Richard, do you miss your dog? He might think it's not a manly enough thing, to miss his dog— do guys in trucks ever think about or realize that they'll probably outlive their dogs? Or do they say, It's just a dog. But if he happened to start a conversation about it or any- thing, she could tell him not to worry if he wanted to miss his dog because Olin cried in his sleep the night after his Dalmatian was hit by a car. She wasn't fast enough, her parents beat her to the door of his room, shoved her back, wouldn't let her in. If he was sixteen she was only six, not a cute little baby to tickle any- more, certainly not mature enough to pay attention to. Can you blame him? But she was wearing make-up and a bra in junior high when he graduated from college and came home for a week before leaving for dental school in Texas. Had already started modeling school when she was seventeen and he came west for their first pasteurized Christmas (without snow) in California, her brownish hair was already jet black and cut like a photo from a French magazine, in stark contrast to the blond clones you see everywhere. Know what? He called her Mouse anyway. Then he and Dad went hunting. She didn't get a chance to sit down with him and talk like two adults. His hair was thinning. She noticed as she stood behind a chair where he was sitting. It was even thinner the next time he came out, for his wedding reception, she was already a professional model, no one called her Mouse, no one called her Glennie either. At any one of the last several reststops she could've put in a call to Olin and described what he should look for: a dirty pick-up truck with big tires and a black roll-bar. Olin'll have some sort of ambulance-chaser attorney who'll slap what's'z'name in jail for the rest of his life, meanwhile Olin'll take her in his arms and weep against her neck. But what if Olin notices she's wearing her own baseball cap, which what's'z'name mentioned he would buy for her. She doesn't want a beer emblem on hers, but in a gas station gift shop she had spotted a white one with a colorful rainbow on the front. Imagine that with her shiny black hair.

Did you ever think you'd be happy to shop for underwear in a dime store? She also got jeans and a cotton blouse—instead of sleeves it has straps that tie over her shoulders, sort of hangs like a loose sack, can't wear a bra with it. She picked up some shampoo too, one of those 49¢ trial sizes. That's all she got in the cosmetics section. He stood by the door and smiled when she came toward him with her bag, and she must've smiled back, maybe without realizing. He wanted to carry the bag for her, but she had to keep it to go into the restroom at the gas station next door and change clothes. He didn't whistle when she came out, just looked. She asked if it had put a big dent into whatever money he had, letting her buy this stuff. He didn't answer for a second. They were already in the truck, pulling out of the gas station. Then she noticed he had a few freckles on his nose. How many guys in trucks do you see with freckles like that? Not dark freckles—the pale unfocused kind like she gets on her shoulders. Right as she was noticing, he said, "Well, it's your money." Of course, he'd taken it from her purse after he'd tied her up after she'd just given his dog shade and water. Maybe if he didn't have those freckles she would've tried to scratch his eyes out right then, for saying how it was her money all along. A lot of her nails have broken along the way and she forgot to buy an emery board. "I never imagined anything like this," he said. "Everything just sort of happened, and you know, I thought, you know, you could've just died on me, gone limp, you know, screamed and carried on, whining, complaining, hysterics, whatever. I mean you could've made me keep you tied and gagged. I'm glad you didn't, for whatever that's worth."

"Are you apologizing?"

"Maybe. Maybe I wish I could." All of a sudden he swerved the truck almost off the road, kicked up sand on the side before getting back into his lane. "It was a snake," he said. "I think it's okay." Guys with trucks don't usually swerve to *miss* snakes. He said, "I guess I wish I could just give you the rest of the money, what's left of it, take you to a bus station or something and let you go on home. I wish I could. Maybe I should. But I'm scared."

"What—you're *scared*?"

"Yeah, I guess so."

"Scared that I'll tell someone and you'll get in trouble?"

"To say the least."

"Scared you'll miss me?"

"Maybe." He never took his eyes off the road. He hadn't taken his eyes off the road much all along, even when tapping her arm with a stick of gum or poking a licorice under her nose. But for a day and a half, hadn't she sat sideways and looked at his profile? Then it was the other way around at night, when she lay on her back and stared at the stars, he lay on his side beside her. The plan in her head was pretty hazy, something about giving the guy Olin's address so he could drop her off there. She'd tell Olin she'd gotten a vacation and had found a free ride to Texas so she came out to get her teeth capped. After all, hadn't he hitchhiked around the country practically every summer when he was in college—that's why she hardly ever saw him. He'd be damn proud of her, and maybe she could even get him to give this guy a couple hundred dollars. "Where're we going?" she asked.

"I don't know. Nowhere in particular. Have any suggestions?"

"Got any more wash-n-drys?"

"In the glove compartment."

"I don't need one right now, just wanted to know where they are."

"Is there anything else you need, really, anything at all?"

She sat there trying to think of something she should ask for. There should've been a million things. He was taking little side glances at her. His eyelashes were long and dark, his ears pinkish like they'd been scrubbed with a paper towel in a reststop restroom. He'd also bought a razor yesterday and shaved in the morning, cut himself on his jawline, not a clean cut but a place where the razor skipped and scraped several times in one stroke. His neck was longer than most necks, and sunburned. His hands not very hairy, but chapped. He needed some medicated skin cream. That's what she thought of asking for. Maybe Olin would have some skin cream. But how could Olin see him like that, as a guy who needed skin cream, Olin wouldn't see any of that. She'd have to say, "Wait, Olin, don't you have anything for his skin?"

She looked down at her new jeans and blouse and plastic sandals. She loved them. For no apparent reason, she took the guy's baseball cap off his head and put it on her own. He smiled, taking his eyes off the road to look at her quickly three or four times, then adjusted the cap so the bill stuck out to the side, swept her black bangs haphazardly away so they were no longer hanging over her eyes.

"There," he said, "that's cute."

"You mean cute like an eight-year-old?"

"Just cute like...cute. Funky-cute."

"Oh, like a puppy dressed in baby clothes!" She sighed and wiped her eyes as though she'd been laughing too hard. He stared at her, then riveted his eyes back

28

on the road.

"You look almost...I don't know...carefree..."

Hey, wait a minute, Olin might think she *wants* to be with this guy in a truck, he might draw conclusions before she can explain, Hey, Olin, it's really your little helpless Mousey, caught and toyed with by this mountain lion, this lynx, this bobcat, this wild tom alleycat, this kitten—really, let me tell you what *happened*!

"Look out," she screamed, "turn, turn, watch out!" She even grabbed the wheel and helped him turn while the breaks squealed, but they'd hit the sand at the side of the road and stopped.

"What," he panted.

"An armadillo, you would've hit it, maybe it's still under the truck, get out and see."

"I didn't hit anything."

"Go on, get out and check, it might be hurt, go on." She even pushed on his shoulder and back as he turned to slide out. If only he'd gotten all the way out, but he slid to the edge of his seat, bent way over so his head hung between his knees and he could see under the truck, upside-down. If she wasn't still wearing his cap, it would've fallen off his head onto the pavement. One more push with both hands made him do a somersault in the street. Hopefully his head was out of the way when she drove off. She could ride into Texas as a bare-assed hood ornament—who was going to notice in a million years if she showed up in Texas with a guy in a truck, or alone in a truck, or at all. She kicked up dust and was gone. Lucky thing the road was straight, she was bawling just enough to make herself blind.

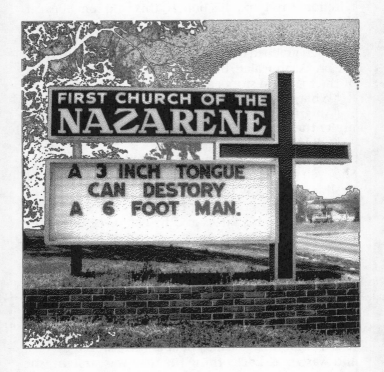

REVELATION COUNTDOWN

The photographer, without any pants, takes a pre-dawn picture of his motel room. But then he winds the film back and re-exposes the frame to destroy the image of the rumpled, soiled sheets. There's no evidence to suggest that someone's breath and heartbeat fluttered against his body all night, like holding a sleeping bird in two cupped hands.

He has a large-format Pentax, 2 lenses (wide and wider), 20 rolls of film, 2 gasoline credit cards, 7 pair of underwear, 9 pair of socks (2 extra if his feet get wet), 14 pears in a cooler, a 2-lb package of carrots, 24 serving-sized cans of V-8 and grapefruit juice, and an AT&T calling card. After a tour of book-signings for his last book of immaculate, comfortable landscape photographs, he's been allotted one free week. Then he'll have to lose the flab (and other foul bad habits) he's been reminded these kinds of trips tend to cause.

1

A cloudbank postpones daybreak. The sun sends a five-pointed star of light through a pinprick hole in the slate-iron sky, spotlighting a lone white mountain between the equally dark desert and foothills. When he's able to turn off the headlights—as the world fades into view, and after he's traveled past the fleecy edges of the overcast—a cloud like a long curved finger zaps down to touch a point on the earth, somewhere beyond the toothy ridge of hills on the horizon. His hand leaves the steering wheel as though to find the camera, but pauses, scratches his head, rests in his lap a moment, then goes back to the wheel.

Just down the block from the gas station phone booth, a portable sign has been wheeled to the sidewalk, an arrow of blinking lights points off the road to a small white church with a tall, needle-thin steeple. The sign's body is opaque fluorescent white, so the plastic letters are sharply conspicuous. The black letters say *Revelation Countdown*, and below that, in red, *world chaos by 7, angels 7:30, Wed. 19th, The road leads to heaven or hell, renounce sins now!* A man is on the other side of the sign, his legs all that are visible, just his feet and ankles. He's changing the message.

Celebrating softly in his chest, only a faint smile on his lips, the photographer frees the camera from its protective padding. The shot is made, the film wound forward. Back to the van, back on the freeway. He eats a box of donuts he picked up at the gas station mini-market, drinks a coke, stuffs the evidence into the brown sack with the damp receipt.

Since the snub-nosed van has no hood poking into his view in front, the big sloping windshield is like living inside his wide-angle lenses. His peripheral vision sharper. If he passed anyone on either shoulder of the freeway, he'd clearly be able to see that expression of disapproval or disappointment.

2

A herd of six deer cross the road in front of him, then stop on the side, turn to stare back at the photographer. His engine idling, his window up, his breath fogs the glass a little, but he wipes it away, takes out the camera, watches the deer through the view finder until they wheel, bolt away, their tails up. Later a coyote runs along the shoulder before veering off into the chaparral. An owl sits on a fence post. At the end of that fence, a long driveway stretches toward a distant house. A sign over the driveway announces live Hereford embryo transfer. A hushed chortle in his throat, the photographer sets up his tripod for the shot. His eye steams up the view-finder. Something like hunger is a tickle in his stomach, and he can smell the sweet cream from his breakfast eclair still on his fingers.

The last few steps back to the van, his loafers are like 50-pound army boots. His clothes feel dank and clammy. Sitting on the rear bumper, he hangs his head but is unable to vomit. He takes a bite of pear. Chews slowly, many times, so he never has to swallow it. Leaves it on the bumper while he walks three and a half times around the van. Washes the windshield and drives on.

3

The salt flats stretch horizon to horizon, punctuated by spots of pale sage, animal holes, rigid quills of grass, four or five shadows of small clouds passing through like migrating animals.

The photographer sits in his van eating a candy bar. Gingerly feels his feet to see if his socks are damp, then slips his loafers back on, carries his camera along, across the freeway to an abandoned motel, licks chocolate from his fingers before taking three or four shots of the empty swimming pool and deck, filmed with a thin layer of snow, marked only by his own footprints walking an undirected looping, criss-crossed pattern around it. Underneath he's smiling at himself for having to step back and use a cable-release so his trembling won't shake the camera. His heart jumps around like something alive in there.

The abandoned motel has a pay phone which still works. Coming back to the van, he sees two or three candy wrappers on the front seat, puts the camera in the van, does ten jumping jacks, watching his face in the window, then opens the door and flops across the seat on his back, his pulse a dull thud, his feet still outside on the freeway shoulder. Watches the air-freshener dangling from the rear-view mirror. Tries to clean his teeth with his tongue. His toes feel slimy. The extra socks were packed for him in a small vinyl suitcase with toothpaste, mouthwash, deodorant, aftershave and shampoo.

4

In the middle of a dry basin, a bare tree stands alone, its many thick branches forking off into many more thinner branches splitting off into thousands of distinctly separate twigs. On the hard ground, the tree's roots look like snakes slithering all over the surface, branching out into a swarm of thinner roots, dividing into a gnarled roadmap of winding trails, crossing each other, winding together, but all heading for the open prairie beyond the shade of the furthest branches.

The photographer leaves his van and walks past the tree before he uncaps the camera, kneels and takes several shots of a family tree etched onto a grave headstone. Lying on the ground, he's under the chilly wind. The hard, bumpy soil is even a little warm, hollows and swells fitting with his body, seems to move with his breath.

The sun on the van's windshield glares in his eyes as he approaches. He digs into the first aid kit for aspirin. Takes a few of the vitamins provided for him as well. Can't seem to get the bandaids, gauze, iodine and cotton swabs packed as neatly as they were in order to close the lid of the box. He shoves it under the seat.

5

The moon is full. It's rising over a little pueblo village, illuminating the walls and roofs as though they're lit from within. But while looking for a public phone, the photographer lets out a mellow chuckle when he finds a bulbous silver water tank rising on stilts in an empty lot beside a fireworks stand. A cartoon tiger swells his chest and flexes his bicep on one side of the silver ball, on the other: *Golden Hill Fighting Tigers*. With his camera on a low tripod, the photographer is on his side, looking up at the resplendent fireworks stand, the glowing water tank hovering above it, a scattering of stars bold enough to stay visible in the velvet sky. He holds his breath, holds his body taut as the shutter opens, then the click is a huge release of air, a flood pouring out of him. He rolls to his back, smiling, sighs and shuts his eyes.

Standing by his van, he takes off one shoe and scratches the bottom of his foot. The restaurant across the street offers a fattening array of chicken-fried steak, homestyle fries, sausage biscuits, peach pie. Maybe he can get a salad. His stomach growls and turns. The sudden chill of night seems to tighten his whole body. He stretches over his head, reaches to touch his toes, stretches again, then takes a deep breath with his hands pressing on his ribs as though they're sore.

He hangs up the phone and curls on his side with a stabbing knot in his stomach. The room smells like perspiration, dirty clothes, stale breath. His snoring sounds like a large insect and wakes him several times as he begins to doze. Later, when the window is grey and the TV in the next room is silent, the photographer wakes. Slowly he stretches his legs out, kicking the scratchy sheets and blanket down, his stomach gently softened, refreshed, as though soothed by someone's generous hand. Or her mouth. Open slightly. Her tongue barely touching, licking his sweat like a kitten lapping whipped cream. He touches himself the same time she does, but neither pulls their hand away in shame. Her whole hand. Her fingertips. A single ardent finger. Then just her breath. He can't tell when she's no longer there. She returns again and again. Like dawn...never shocking, always astonishing...not ever methodical, always natural...never fragile, always delicate...and yet somehow extraordinarily untamed.... When it's still before sunrise, she'll be waiting for him on the bed with wet slicked-down hair, jeans and torn sneakers, smiling as he puts on yesterday's socks, yesterday's pants; then they'll go exploring at a time when the air is still as much water as it is light, like the touch of her mouth still damp on his skin.

6

So at midmorning, he relishes a hotdog in the parking lot of the DipDog drive-thru. Wipes his fingers on the leg of his pants. The DipDog sign is a fat arrow, high on a post, drooping to point down at the tiny food stand which is steaming from its windows and several spots in its roof. A juicy scent of the hotdogs being grilled, a tint of mustard and onions in the crisp air. He takes his shot of the DipDog sign, then returns to the van to touch himself, wetting his fingers on his tongue, touching again, his chest and nipples and soft stomach, and his penis. Then takes another shot of the DipDog arrow.

7

In the restroom at the Kuntry Kitchen, the condom machine is illustrated with a drawing of a woman in high-cut lace underwear and push-up bra, her back arched, knees half bent, a hand on her hip, head turned and leering over one shoulder. The machine offers "The Screamer." The words under the illustration say, "If she's a moaner, it'll make her a screamer. If she's a screamer, it'll get you arrested."

Beside the condom machine is a cologne dispenser. Drop in a quarter, press a button and position yourself to be squirted by your favorite scent: DRAKKAR, POLO or STAG MUSK.

The photographer leans against a wall, bracing himself to steady the camera, and gets a shot of the two machines. If someone came light-footed through the door to join him...her reckless laugh, her bold hands touching the machine as though reading it by braille....

He buys a condom, puts it in his pocket. Stands aside and lets each of the three colognes shoot into the room. Mixes the air with one hand, then walks through the cool mist.

8

The morning newspaper from someplace in Idaho carries a story about a man arrested for masturbating in a rest stop restroom. A state trooper had followed him into the restroom, observed him through a crack in the door. The man refused the trooper's offer to go to a motel room and was then arrested for infamous crimes against nature. The photographer rips the article out of the paper. At the first rest stop he comes to, the photographer pulls off. He pauses on his way to the men's room at a row of eight or ten pay phones. Every phone except one is occupied by a truck driver, the smallest around 200 pounds. All in cowboy or baseball hats, jeans, plaid shirts, boots, sweaty hair. Broken pieces of technical truck language can be heard under the freeway roar. The empty phone is in the middle. Someone else *could* dash up to use that middle phone, half the size of any of the truckers surrounding her, leaning luxuriantly against the box, listening only to the dial tone as she touches her stomach below her short T-shirt with two unrestrained fingers which then dig below the waistband of her jeans and reappear to slip between her lips. He takes a picture, laughing. Then moves on. Takes a roll of tape from his camera bag and goes into a toilet stall with his camera. He tapes the article to the door, sits on the toilet, uncaps his camera, unzips his pants. She waits outside, squatting in the shade beside the building, drawing in the dirt with a stick or sitting on top of the posted state roadmap, tapping her heels against Boise or Twin Falls. When he comes out, she'll take his hands and touch between his fingers with her tongue, close her eyes, hold his sticky palms to her cheeks.

9

The last five frames in his camera hold another church

sign: *Our Preacher Speaks: a.m. An Empty Field, p.m. Under the Pulpit*. In a Wyoming 8-room motel, the photographer looks at the phone beside the bible on the nightstand. Goes to the jukebox joint next door. Dark with blinking lights and tinkling conversation. The photographer sits watching the television behind the bar. The two cowboys on his right have selected a car race. The photographer's eyes go round and round with the speeding cars. The beer is fresh in his mouth. The salty peanuts alive on his tongue.

The bar atmosphere is quickened as a huge Indian with long black hair, turquoise kerchief and leather chaps comes in, pelted by shouts of welcome and invitations to share a pitcher of beer. But the Indian gets his own pitcher, sits on the photographer's left, watches the television for a moment, then asks the bartender if he could change the channel. The bartender looks at the two cowboys. They shrug, put their mugs to their mouths. The Indian stands, leans across the bar. His arms are enormously long. He reaches over the bar, past the bartender, above the bottles lining the counter and spins the dial. The Indian settles back as an old Bogart movie flickers on the screen. Someone heading toward the restrooms pauses behind the Indian, says something, calls him Snake, her hand unabashed on the back of his neck, under his hair. The Indian shows small white teeth when he smiles. During an ad, he says, "On vacation?" He's looking at the photographer.

"Not exactly. In a way, I guess."

"Take a vacation any way it comes," the Indian says. "That's how to do it. Five minutes. Ten. Anything you can get."

"Well, I'm just sort of coasting toward home."

The Indian smiles. "I saw you today, taking a picture of the Wilson Brothers Ranch sign."

"Don't worry. I'm not a developer or insurance adjuster."

"Anyone can take a picture of a cow," the Indian says. "But that sign…the longer it stands out there, the rust running down is giving that metal bull a pretty fine set of testicles."

The photographer smiles, pushing a palmful of peanuts into his mouth.

"You oughta try the taxidermy shop across the street," the Indian says. "There's some wildlife photos for you."

As the photographer is saying, "Thanks, I will," the atmosphere peaks again as three or four uniformed men come in, move deliberately to the bar, standing behind the Indian and on both sides of him, squeezing the photographer away. With his arms pinned behind his back, they lift the Indian from his stool and take him outside. The photographer pays for his beer and follows, but when he gets to the door, one of the uniformed men is there, shakes his head. "I can't go?" the photographer says.

"Not yet."

"I have to make a call."

"Phone's there." The man nods toward the restrooms. The sounds coming from outside are muffled thuds, low grunts, grinding and shuffling of feet on the gravel parking lot. Then a low whistle. The uniformed man says, "Okay, it's all over," and leaves in front of the photographer. The Indian is spread-eagle over the trunk of a car, then is put into the back seat and pushed over so he's no longer visible. The car leaves. Broken glass gleams in the parking lot under the yellow lights.

He wakes far past dawn, sheets soaked, but doesn't take time to shower or use the phone before taking his camera across the street to the taxidermy shop.

10

The taxidermist, with skin like tanned leather, doesn't speak. Stands behind the counter with level eyes locked on the photographer. The glass eyes of every stuffed creature in the shop focus to a point in the middle of the counter, where a customer would stand at the cash register paying for a stuffed memory.

The photographer says, with a brittle laugh, "Hey, is this where people come to become stuffed-shirts?"

"Job's been done." Any one of the glassy-eyed heads could've said it. The taxidermist's mouth hadn't moved.

"What season is it?" the photographer asks. "What are they hunting right now?"

The taxidermist doesn't answer, but the voice, now obviously coming from a dark back room, says, "Stray tourists."

The taxidermist stays parallel with the photographer as he moves to look more closely at a stuffed trout mounted on a board, its body arched, head and tail pointing down, mouth open in a silent moment of unvanquished excitement—except for the hook left in its jaw. As the photographer reaches to touch the fish, the taxidermist pulls it a little further back on the counter. Not entirely out of reach, but the photographer's hand stops.

"You know what they say," the photographer says, "nothing's certain but death and taxidermy."

The taxidermist's thin lips don't move, but again the disembodied voice from behind: "In some cases, you can't tell which happened first."

The photographer tries to look behind the taxidermist through a partially opened door in the back of the shop. A man's shoulder, part of the back of his head, his arms moving, doing something with what could be the wing of a large, stiff bird.

The taxidermist blocks the photographer's view. The photographer's eyes roam to all the stuffed heads along the walls behind the counter, on the beam above the counter, eight-pointed stags, heavy-horned rams, birds in flight. When he's finished looking, another man is standing beside the taxidermist behind the counter, wearing an identical leather apron, also staring at the photographer. The second man's head is huge, without hair. He says, "Too much fat, not enough meat."

The photographer edges away to the side wall where a bulletin board is filled with a patchwork of greenish Polaroid photos of hunters and their trophies. Eyes closed, the big-horned sheep could be sleeping with its chin resting on the hunter's knee. The photographer stares at each polaroid for several moments, lingering longest over one of what appears to be a swan, the hunter holding the wings spread out in front of himself, a six-foot span, the elegant neck flapping limp against its breast. His eyes return to it again and again,

43

two of his fingers pinching and tugging on his lower lip. The first taxidermist comes out from behind the counter. Wipes dust from the nostril of a stag elk. The second taxidermist says, "Those loafers'll be needing to be polished again *real* soon."

The photographer jumps when the first taxidermist pinches the flesh above his belt.

A truck pulls into the gravel lot outside. Then another. Several others. Doors slam. Loud laughter. The first one, coming through the door backwards, pushes the photographer out of the way with the butt of the deer slung across his shoulders. An elbow in his stomach. Someone steps on his feet. Another and another come in with animals across their backs. Blood-soaked white bellies or shot through the eye. Antlers clacking, boots shuffling, the smell of fur and musk as still more hunters push through the door wearing their kill on their backs. The photographer backs up against a wall, the taxidermist still beside him, still holding onto his love-handle, still silent. The other taxidermist is circulating among the hunters, measuring antler racks, examining entry wounds, tagging ears. The tip of an antler scratches the photographer's cheek. He can't move. They start stacking the carcasses against the walls, three high, knee deep, legs tangled on the floor, boots shuffling in mud and dried blood. A big guy in a red plaid shirt hoists his pants higher and belches, then asks if anyone's seen Straight Snake, that boozing bastard, fucking wives while the men are on a weekend hunt and all they've had is deer cunt. As the mob swirls among the dead deer, the big guy stops in front of the photographer, "Don't worry, sweetheart, I'll give her a big kiss for you." The guy's cracked, cold lips are on the photographer's, his beef-jerky breath inside the photographer's mouth, his hand grabbing the front of the photographer's pants. The animal smell is thick and feral, there's blood on the photographer's shirt, but the men are leaving, stopping traffic to cross the road to the jukebox joint where the parking-lot gravel contains human teeth. When the taxidermist lets go of his flap of flab, the photographer edges sideways out the door.

He gets up before dawn to unplug the phone and open the window. Cold clean air rushing in to meet festering air in the room could cause a storm. His rank breath. Rancid sweat. He returns to the bed and lays facing away from the window, feeling a breath come like a feathery touch over his shoulder and back. As though she came through the window in the wind. Fits herself behind him. Half his size, but holding him, breathing his air deeply into her body, her hands tender on his soft waist. Her heartbeat resuscitates his.

But he's within one day's drive of home and it'll be his move, after all, which sends her back out the window.

In all, it only took him five days to get home. On the outskirts of town, he stops. One at a time pulls all 9 remaining pair of socks onto his feet, peels them off, stuffs them into the folded laundry bag. Throws away all hotdog, hamburger, and candy wrappers, all coke cans, all donut boxes, all gum papers. Finishes his last film toward a distant dusty mountain range, a hundred miles on each frame, from north to south.

He sits at the formica kitchen table eating meatloaf and peas. His shirt smells cottony. From the utility room, the slosh of the washer, hum of the drier. Scent of bleach. Powdery taste of fabric softener. He looks out the kitchen window, but it's dark and he only sees the reflection of a kitchen with a photographer looking out. But it's not nighttime—it's because the hedge, which needs monthly clipping, has grown above the window. He stands to see over the leaves, chewing his last bite of meatloaf, looking into the back yard where an old bicycle has been taken out of the attic and turned into an exercycle for him, its rear wheel propped up, unable to get anywhere, no matter how hard or fast the pedals are pumped.

NOT HERE

The girl told him about a river in Wisconsin...clear and guileless, cold and honest, and some asshole like you or me standing on the bank somewhere, slitting open a fish, dumping the guts. But that's where he went, three weeks every year, for ten years. Ever since she had said, "Pretty nifty sneakers, Mister Fisherman...they'll look great with a grey suit." And then a few hours later, "Say what you mean, you coward, you bastard."

His very first time out, he'd almost landed a 20 lb. brown trout in a pool at the foot of a short falls. What an incredible pumping sensation, the 5 or 10 seconds he'd had that thing on the line. But that fish was long gone, dead, caught by someone else, fried, or turned to mulch on the muddy bank of the river. And the girl never even heard about it. He didn't really continue to believe he'd be able to go back and hook into the same one in the same pool—some years shallower, some years overflowing and creating a marsh so he couldn't get near enough to get his bait into the deepest holes.

❖

Does anyone ever call you Ronnie?

Sometimes my mother does.

I wouldn't ever call you Ronnie, but in these movies that's what you are—Ronnie. Lookit that face, Jeez-Louise, you poor kid, going on vacation with a bunch of adults. Didja ever get to hold the fishing pole yourself?

I think so.

Don't you remember?

Not really. I remember we went to Florida. And Galveston. And Las Vegas. Mostly we went to Las Vegas. But this was before it was such a big deal. There was a little amusement park across the street from our hotel. I went there every day.

By yourself?

Yeah.

Poor little Ronnie, always on vacation with the adults, no kids to play with.

I've got you to play with now.

But you're still going on those adult vacations, aren't you? Some bus tour through New England sitting beside Mr. and Mrs. Booth from Duluth.

You take me on a non-adult vacation. Where would we go?

It's not where that's important—but how. Walk around Greenwich Village at 3 a.m. The coast of Maine at dawn. Or...you think you've been fishing? Forget three days of drinking beer and trolling for one stuffed trophy. Stand in a glacier river up to your thighs.

Brrr.

No, you'd be addicted. Didja know when you cook a fresh-caught trout, it curls up and tries to swim outta the pan?

How do you know?

I've done it! You held your mother's hand and walked on the beach in pants and shoes; I was two eyes looking outta a layer of woodsmoke and mud, wet to my knees all day, blood all over my hands—either mine or a fish's—fingernails caked with salmon eggs. That's why I don't like caviar. I always want to take it off the silver platter and bait-up my hook.

Yeah, I can't take you anywhere, can I?

You think that's funny?

From Indianapolis, he could get almost anywhere in the same amount of time, give or take a day or two. Maybe it was time to try somewhere else. Besides, he wanted to avoid the stock truck. Ten years ago, it had all been just like she'd described it…the fishy smell of stagnant mud, slosh of icy water in his sneakers, flash of silver scales under bright shallow rapids, sharp gills cutting his fingers, the roar of the falls and his heartbeat in his ears. But the fish farms and stock trucks made the sensation more and more difficult to find: dumping hundreds of stunned grain-fed monsters into the river from a bridge, screaming children running down the road with too-expensive rods and reels, mothers with nets letting their toddlers scoop the dazed fish from the shallow inlets where they'd been carried by the current.

Last year he saw two women on the opposite side of

the river, both in dresses and heels. They'd pulled their car off the road and were standing there fishing from the unlikely position of a bluff which was 6 or 8 feet above the bank of the river. He'd heard their shrieks every 5 or 10 minutes, looked up to see them flip another huge, shining rainbow trout out of the water, sling it over their heads so it flopped in the dust near the front tires of their car. Then they threw a gunny sack over it, somehow released the hook, added the fish to the bleeding load in their ice chest, and put the can't-miss treble hook loaded with salmon eggs back into the water.

He lay awake that night listening to the river, hearing as well the car radios and laughter around camp-fires. He couldn't close his eyes without seeing his bait disappear under a riffle, then feeling the strike and the struggle, his heart racing, his legs going weak like softened wax, even his fingertips buzzing. Maybe what those screaming women had felt was the same as the tug in his heart, the gush of adrenaline in his guts at the moment of the bang-bang-bang of the strike.

Sometimes, even now after catching thousands of fish, it seemed like he hadn't had that feeling in years.

D'you remember anything about fishing on that boat with your father and uncles?

No. Not really.

Okay, we'll have to start at the beginning. This is a hook.

Well, I know that much.

D'you know how to tie it on?

I guess not.

I'll show you. See how small this hook is? You don't need it any bigger. See this one? That's a treble-hook. That's only for kids under five and real dweebs.

Why?

Can't miss with a treble hook. Fish can't steal the bait. Any way he hits it, he's caught. You can pay me back for this, you know.

What do you mean?

You can teach me things. Like which fork to use in a restaurant.

It doesn't matter a lot.

I watched you last night, I did what you did.

How do you know I used the right fork?

I trust you.

Ellen used to scold me for using the same fork for the whole meal. But I wasn't trying to be a snob by taking you to a place with fifteen forks. The food's good there.

Yeah. Well, that spinach thing had too much butter.

Florentine.

Yeah, that. It had too much butter.

I'm sorry, I sounded like a snob again.

No, how the hell am I gonna learn what these fancy dishes are if you don't tell me. I can't be a chef and go on making something called spinach-thing or crab-thing or veal-named-after-a-king-thing.

You're going to be a chef?

I decided last night.

❖

53

He wasn't even to Champaign yet. Why not, instead of spending 3 weeks fishing in Wisconsin, go ahead and take 3 or 4 extra days and drive to Southern Louisiana. Stop in Tennessee or Arkansas on the way, catch a few, take snapshots, no one would be the wiser *where* he'd caught his fish. He always had to have snapshots of the day's catch or the largest...and took pictures of signs to show where he'd been. Gail, his second wife, flipped through the pictures and always said the same thing, "Well, I'm glad the trip was relaxing and good for your nerves. Maybe you won't be so edgy for a while now." She liked to stay at home by the pool. They'd been next door neighbors in the apartment complex. Living together and then getting married had just seemed to happen.

Darcy. She liked her own name. She didn't color her hair. She wore no make-up. There was a raccoon mask around her eyes from wearing sunglasses. A scar on her chin from a dogbite. She didn't wear nail polish. Clipped her nails short. Weighed 100 pounds but could lift a 40 lb sack of dog food and carry it from her truck to the storeroom of the kennel. And could do more things with an egg than he'd ever had the imagination to hunger for. She wore no perfume but smelled of spices when she'd been cooking. He used Darcy's father's kennel to board his first wife's dog when they went on trips.

Gail spent a month every year at a country-club health resort. He'd gone with her a few times, at first. It was never the same month as his fishing trip. She asked why he didn't go fishing while she was at the club, if he hated going there so much. He said he didn't hate it. He

54

always said things like that instead of answering.

He pulled into a two-pump gas station in Cooks Mills. A woman was getting off a Greyhound bus. A man got out of a sedan, took two suitcases from the bus driver, put them into the trunk of the sedan then got back into the car behind the wheel. The woman turned and looked at the bus. The bus driver didn't wave. The bus pulled between Ron and the woman. After the bus went past and pulled out onto the road, the woman was already inside the car with the man. She had her head tipped back over the seat.

Darcy was a chef now in a restaurant in New Orleans. He'd almost left his first wife for her, a long time ago, ten years ago. He'd left his wife anyway, but it was too late. Three or four years too late. The girl was gone. To New Orleans. She'd written him sad letters once a month for a year and a half. He always intended to answer, but there never seemed to be the right thing to say. By the time he finally did leave his marriage, the last correspondence—a postcard of geese flying in formation between two blank billboards on a two-lane highway, with her printed message saying simply, *more later*—was at least two years old.

DiCarlo's? Is this a boarding facility?

Yeah, about once a week some ding-dong calls here for a pizza. Whadda *you* want? I mean, can I help you?

I'm going to England. My wife's dog has to be boarded.

Wife's dog? So *you're* not gonna claim it?

It's a Pomeranian.

I don't blame you. You look like you should own...a spaniel.

Why?

That suit—I'll bet you didn't pick it out. Someone who owns a Pomeranian chose that suit. You'd probably like to put on a red plaid flannel shirt and jeans and go wet your line in a creek somewhere.

Do you speak to all your customers this way?

Just certain ones—when I think it's worth my while. Besides, you got lucky, my father's not here today.

Hey...put your foot up here.

Why?

Your shoe's untied.

So it is. I'd make a great impression stepping on it and falling on my face.

Put your foot up here.

Careful you don't get your finger caught in the knot.

He stayed on back roads, so he could stop and take pictures of places he might've fished. Bucksnort Trout Pond in Tennessee. Catch-a-Rainbow Bait-n-Tackle in Arkansas. Pioneer River Fishing Resort in Texas. He was zig-zagging, but heading south. He drove down Louisiana between 11 p.m. and 6 a.m. The yellow diamond-shaped highway signs illuminated by his headlights all said "Church" instead of things like "Icy" or "Slow Trucks." Maybe there aren't any slow trucks where there are a lot of churches. Everything was totally dark except those signs and the on-coming truck headlights in the distance. When they passed, they almost blew him off the road. The gear in his tackle box rattled.

Hey, Ron, I got a great idea.
Tell me.
Let me cater your family Thanksgiving.
You've got to be kidding. My in-laws will be there, my wife's sister and her family. There's no way—
Hey, I can cook, can't I? I could put it on my resumé, that I catered a big Thanksgiving bash for a prominent lawyer.
I'm not prominent. I'm pretty average.
Just think of it, Ron, you could come into the kitchen and catch the cook bending over, basting the turkey, with nothing on but an apron—and get basted yourself at the same time. Start a new holiday tradition.
I'll never feel the same about gravy.

❖

At the intersection where an uphill off-ramp became a downhill on-ramp—after crossing the service road which went over the interstate—a man was standing on a rock in the rain watching cars on the freeway through a massive pair of binoculars. The street was slick and shiny. The tires hissed. The man's wet clothes whipped in the wind like flags on a pole.

Fishing can be good in the rain because the fish can't look up through the disturbed surface of the water and see the murky movement of the fisherman. Most years he got at least one rainfall during his trip, but not last year. The trip had been put off a month because his mother visited, so it was too late into the summer. A thunderstorm always made the river seem quieter, softer. Wet clothes were never uncomfortable. Of course, daytime noise of campers also made the river seem smaller and the splashing rumble less loud. But before dawn, there was usually just the crunch of his footsteps and roar of the swift water. That was the time of day, just last year, when he came into the clearing beside the small waterfall that tumbled into a deeper pool. A girl was sitting on the ground, untying her shoe, taking out the shoelace and using it to string together her morning's catch of three trout. As the white lace passed through the gills, it came out bloody red. Blood trickled down the side of one fish, dripping from its twitching tail. Darcy would be over 30 by now.

So, does just one guy cook all these things?

There's usually a head chef. I'm not sure. Maybe a lot of apprentices. I've never been in the kitchen before.

Let's ask if we can go see!

It's kind of busy right now.

I wanna know who puts the parsley on...*just* right. And who decided to put mustard in this sauce.

How could you tell?

Taste it!

I did. I wouldn't've been able to name the ingredients.

I'd cut back on the dill weed too.

Not here, Darcy.

Huh?

Your hand, not here.

Oh. Sorry. Hey, can you leave work early tomorrow? We can go to the fly casting practice pond in the park.

I thought you preferred live bait.

I do. It seems more fair, cause if you're not good enough, at least the fish gets some food as his reward for winning and getting away.

Do you feel bad when that happens?

Bad? Not bad. Excited, trembling, pumped, high...then suddenly the line goes slack and you don't know what to do with all that energy except go for it again. Hey, how do you think people get to be apprentices to a chef or something?

I don't know. Ask. Apply. Send out resumés. Bring in a baked Alaska.

Yeah, like: here's my portfolio! Pull a dish of shrimp scampi out of a briefcase.

Darcy—not here.

Oh, Jesus. I can't keep my hands off you, can I. I'm just so excited thinking about being a chef. D'you think I should go to chef school or try to get hired as an assistant and work my way up? I tend to prefer just doing it. Hey, whadda you think those people over there are eating? Am I talking too loud?

A man in a sleek red car pulled into the rest stop but didn't park nor turn the engine off. He was speaking into a walkie talkie. A streamline black car pulled alongside. The man in the red car spoke to the people in the black car, laughing, his face open with joy. The woman beside him in the red car stared straight ahead, unsmiling, her profile a sharp cut-out against the tinted window on her other side. The man's excited words and laughter sounded like someone across the river, shouting to a buddy and holding up a silver trout, its body twisting back and forth, throwing arcs of water from its flashing tail. The woman put two fingers on each of her temples. Her hair was an elaborate, frosted shape.

When you feel the strike, set the hook. Don't let it swallow the bait. If you set the hook right, the fish won't be hurt much—you can let it go and catch it again tomorrow.

How will I know— What does a strike feel like?

God, that's like asking what chocolate tastes like, what pine trees smell like...what a kiss feels like...it only feels like what it feels like, there's no other way to describe it.

Try. I'd like to hear you try.

Okay...Bang. It feels like *bang*.

Like a gunshot?

No. Silent. No pain. Like your heart breaking open.

That's not pain?

Like the happiest time in your life all squished down into two seconds. *Bang*.

I've never had a conversation like this before.

Why? Am I drunk? D'you get me to talk about stupid stuff when I'm drinking just so it'll be funny and different and a few yuks to pass along to your lawyer buddies?

C'mon, Darcy. It's just a fun conversation. Hey, I don't get to talk to anyone like this.

But do you tell your friends about me?

No. I don't talk about you. I don't tell anyone about you.

Why? Ashamed?

No...well, maybe, in a way. I wouldn't be able to describe you. They'd get the wrong idea and I'd be ashamed of *that*.

You can't describe me? C'mon, try.

I don't know. I couldn't describe you to anyone and make you seem real. It wouldn't be the whole you. They'd wonder what the hell I was doing with you.

Well, hey, should I be insulted? No, I guess it's *their* problem. But could you describe how I make you feel?

Bang.

I like that! Let them misunderstand that one!

Anything I said would be misinterpreted unless someone knew you.

Try. C'mon, try. Let's hear it. I'll be some fat bald lawyer you've taken out for a...what's that word ...*upscale*...some upscale lunch...steak for lunch. Steak and french fries and 2 pieces of lettuce they call a salad. Is that pretty typical?

I guess.

So, okay, impress me with your extra-curricular exploits. Who's this girl you're seeing? What's she like?

She...uh...okay, she told me how to scrape the blood out of a fish's spine with the back of a thumb-nail...and...she taught me how to tie flies...and she ...she'll have to learn not to lick her fingers while she cooks if she ever becomes a gourmet chef...and she always wants to mess up my hair at the wrong time ...and...dogs listen to her and love her and respond to every inflection in her voice, every tiny signal of her body language...and...and she comes and comes and comes when I fuck her. God, I've never talked like this to a woman before.

Something wrong with it?

No, I like it.

❖

A girl wearing a black leotard and overalls hopped out of a small truck. The overall straps were unhooked, trailing behind her. The bib was a loincloth flapping in front. She had a camera, squatted and took a picture of a single stock of red-gold wheat grass, standing in front of and framed by the hollow burned-out trunk of a still-living tree. The grass had its fleecy head bowed, lacy arms outstretched. The girl went back to her truck, returned without the camera, carrying a tennis racket. After a forehand smash, backhand, and answer with the forehand, the wheat grass was no longer there. She picked shards of fiber from the face of the tennis racket. Then she climbed back into the cab, one of the overall straps dangling out, but she slammed the door on it and drove off, the buckle trolling the pavement beneath the truck.

❖

Darcy, I have to remind you...we won't be the only

two people in this place.

And?

Just remember that. It's different than when we're alone.

Oh yeah, no public displays of affection. Got it.

I've always been this way, Darcy, it's not just you. I don't think it's right for people to hang all over each other in public places.

Do I hang on you?

Well...yes, sometimes you're a cuddly little thing.

In public, Ron, in public, do I hang on you? Have I ever *hung* on you?

No, I guess not.

You see, I know how to behave. You may think I don't know what's proper, but I do. I was raised *proper*...in Texas. That's why I can cook a meal with whatever ingredients I'm given...that's why I can take stains out of underwear.... You think I don't know how to behave?

No, I think you probably do.

I'll tell you how proper my behavior is. Two years after I graduated from high school, before we moved up here, I sent a sympathy card to my old high school principal when his wife died. He wouldn't've even known me, but I knew what was proper. Don't you think that was proper, Ron?

Yes, it was proper.

Yeah, then my principal was arrested and convicted of killing her.

Really? Did you know he'd killed her?

Of course not. If I'd known, I would've sent one of my all-occasion cards.

❖

At the counter, a woman was buying *People* magazine, Lifesavers, chocolate cupcakes, prunes, mixed nuts, beef jerky, and toilet paper. While the clerk waited for the money, she turned and called out the door, "Want anything, Chuck?" The clerk waited. The woman left the counter, stood in the doorway. A huge Winnebago was parked in the closest slot. She shouted, "Hey, Chuck, whadda you want?" The driver of the Winnebago had his head down on his arms on the steering wheel, his face tucked in. The woman was wearing baggy red shorts. The fronts of her thighs were burned pink and clashed with the shorts.

❖

Wow—good thing you wanted me to wear a dress.

Well, I read this place is supposed to have one of the top ten chefs in the world. I thought you'd like to taste the best—know what you're shooting for.

Haven't you ever been here before?

No.

Why not?

No occasion, I guess.

What's the occasion now?

I don't know. That I got you to wear a dress?

Ho ho. You'll pay for that later.

How?

Maybe...by coming up from behind me, lifting the back of this damn skirt and making me bend over.

D'you think anyone's had a conversation like this

in here before?

Has anyone ever done anything like *this* in here before?

Ooh— Maybe that's why they put the napkins over our laps.

Hey Ron...I notice you didn't tell me not to do stuff like that in public.

And you forgot about proper behavior.

When you've got a hard-on, it's only proper for me to touch it, isn't it?

Jeez, I can't believe we're talking like this in here.

Well, we could leave and go to this place I know of— it has plastic placemats with fall-colored leaves on one side and green Christmas trees on the other.

If you're rich enough—and in a place like this it's taken for granted—there are two things you're considered incapable of doing: pulling out and pushing in your own chair and unfurling a napkin and putting it on your own lap.

I had mine done before they got to me.

Sometimes a particular current, swirling around a rock, felt like a bite. Or the bait hitting a submerged log—that felt like a bite. But nothing on earth could really be similar to the real thing, the strike. It couldn't be shared, it couldn't be felt watching someone else get it. Once another guy with a canvas fishing vest was working the other side of the river and stopped just opposite him. The other guy caught 2 fish while Ron felt nothing on his line. His bait insisted on drifting back into a stagnant place. He kept lifting it out, tossing it toward the spot where he saw the other guy hook his two fish. But he never saw nor heard nor felt the other guy's strike. There was just suddenly the whirr of the other's reel, the gentle swishing splash of the fish being drawn toward shore, and a rustle in the grass as the guy held the fish down on the ground to remove the hook.

His worst year fishing was last year when he'd had to move his trip from early June to mid July because his mother was visiting from Seattle. The stock truck came and dumped fish twice a week. Up and down the river, children could be found at almost every decent hole pulling the whale-sized trout out of the river with treble hooks or nets or even by hand. He'd been under the bridge once, standing in waders three feet from the shore. The road above him rumbled, a truck door slammed. He looked up and saw the bulging net of wet silver fins and sleek twisting bodies. "Hold your hat out," the stock truck man yelled. "Here's what you're waiting for!" The fish splashed into the water all around him. A few hit his body first then bounced off into the river. Just after that he'd thought he was getting a bite, tried to set the hook but the bait came flying out of the water, hit his face and the hook nicked the corner of his eye.

The night before his mother had gone home, he'd needed to go to the store and get hooks, line and salmon eggs. Gail had grabbed her purse and said, "I'm coming with you. I need a few things."

"At a sporting goods store?"

"I've got to get out of here," she whispered. "She's driving me crazy. Thank god she doesn't try to visit during the holidays."

On the way home Gail wanted to stop and get hamburgers at a fast food restaurant, eat them there, then go home and tell his mother they didn't feel like having dinner that night.

"I think she wants me to bring back a pizza," he said.

"Are you going to do whatever she asks?"

"I don't mind pizza. What's wrong with pizza?"

"Well, I don't want any pizza," Gail said. "Let's just tell her we already ate."

"I'm hungry."

"Then stop here for hamburgers. Or how about fish and chips. She doesn't have to know. Then we can say we're not hungry and we're not going to eat."

Gail had stayed in the bedroom while Ron and his mother shared the pizza and watched TV. The next day his mother's plane went back to Seattle and Ron packed his car for his fishing trip. Gail watched and said, "If it's warmer there this time of year, I wouldn't mind going with you." He said, "I don't know if it's warmer, I've never been this time of year."

"It's got to be warmer," she said.

"You can never tell," he said.

Gail walked away but came back with a paper towel and began washing the car's mirrors. The heels on her sandals clicked on the driveway. She said, "Wouldn't it be fun to teach me to fish?"

Ron slammed the trunk. The paper towel in Gail's hand wasn't wadded in a ball. She had folded it into a square. "I'm leaving right now," he'd said.

He parked in an empty parking lot in front of a big dark Big Deal store in Alexandria, Louisiana. There were only 2 lights on poles in the parking lot. The street was unlit and none of the houses or buildings had lights in the windows or over the porches. Perhaps people moved into town in the morning and left it at night. He was still sitting up, his head back against the seat. It was around three a.m. His sleeping bag was unrolled and unzipped, spread around him and tucked under his chin. The car thermometer said it was 30 degrees outside. He reclined the seat a little but could still see out the windshield. A man and a woman with quiet footsteps were walking through the parking lot. They were not touching each other. They passed right in front of the car. The woman's hair was long, down her back, blowing slightly in the breeze. She watched the ground as she walked. When she stopped to pick something up, the man kept walking. She put whatever it was into her pocket then hurried a little to catch up. The man said, "I saw that. Whaddaya want that for?" The woman took whatever it was out of her pocket again, then it fluttered down from her hand and they kept walking.

❖

Wait a minute, Darcy.

No. I've heard enough.

C'mon, you're over-reacting, I didn't say—

You don't have to say anything else, Ron. Waiting for the dog to die is perfectly understandable.

It's just a saying. It didn't mean anything.

Then say what you mean.

I don't know what I mean.

Where're my shoes? These're yours.
Darcy…. What'd you do to your hand?
Nothing.
There's blood on it.
Oh. I didn't notice. The dogs were barking. I put my fist through the window.
Why?
The dogs were barking.
That's not the reason.
Maybe not.

❖

He walked around downtown New Orleans in his khaki fishing vest and plaid shirt, high top sneakers and jeans. He paused to read the posted menu of each big restaurant. Most required coat and tie. Two girls came out of the Bon Ton Cafe in shorts and cotton blouses, sunglasses on their heads, toenails painted pink. They smiled at him. A poodle on a leash was sniffing his shoes, then lifted its leg and peed while its blue-haired owner read the Bon Ton menu. The girls laughed and crossed the street. The old lady apologized. "I think my shoes smell like fish," Ron said. Gail usually washed everything, including the shoes, when he got home. But last year he'd tied the shoes together by the laces and hung them with his kreel. They were the same shoes he'd worn on his first fishing trip. He only wore them fishing. He'd worn them once to DiCarlo's boarding kennel. Darcy had left blood fingerprints on them, but after his first fishing trip he hadn't been able to tell if the blood was still there. She'd been holding a shoe in each hand, her pants pulled up but unzipped and gaping open, her underwear was white, her belt unthreaded and hanging down to her ankles, blood smeared across one of her hands, holding his shoes. She let the shoes drop, but not all the way. The laces slipped through her fingers. The shoes dangled in front of her, she held each by the tip of a lace, between thumb and forefinger. Then the shoes thumped on the floor, Darcy turned, he lunged and caught her hanging belt, she grabbed it in both fists and whipped it out of his hands, dragging him halfway off the bed before he finally let go.

NOT THE END OF THE WORLD

We were on our way to Arkansas. A friend who'd moved to Marked Tree thought if I visited, I might consider moving my business there. Marked Tree Landscaping had a ring. Lisa said she wasn't sure she wanted to go, but it wasn't too hard to talk her into it. Nothing unusual, she whined but gave in.

On those long stretches of desert in California and Arizona, it seemed that all she wanted to talk about was her childhood. I hadn't known she had gone to an all-white school for 11 years until they had to integrate. Her mother told her not to use the restrooms and to never touch the handrails on the stairs to the second floor. I realized I was actually with someone who'd used the word "nigger" up until she was sixteen.

"It was a long time ago," she said, trying to get me to stop laughing. She wouldn't laugh. She said it hurt.

For a long time she'd kept saying she was sick and wouldn't let me visit. Almost too long. I kept wondering when she was going to go get it taken care of. She finally saw a doctor. But since she'd already taken so much time off, they fired her from the all-night store.

So I suggested she could come along while I scouted out the new territory. I hadn't even known she grew up back there, Virginia. I hadn't been with her 24 hours a day before the trip.

At first she said, "But it's such a hot, miserable drive."

"Not in January," I said.

She said, "You mean that desert cools down sometimes?"

"It'll freeze your ass off sometimes."

There's a place between El Centro and Yuma where the sand dunes have nothing growing in them and they ripple like waves, like it was another planet where sand is water. I saw her looking at the sand, so I told her I'd read that they came out there to film part of a Star Wars movie. She didn't stop looking at the dunes, and said, "That was a nice movie, wasn't it?"

"*Nice*?" I said. I'd seen it three times.

It was hard for her to rest because we were in my economy truck and the seats didn't recline. I'd taken my landscape tools out of the truckbed and had gotten a cheap camper shell to cover our suitcases and her dog, Tracy, who was riding back there. I remember seeing the dog in her apartment, and she would call it kiddo or brat, but during the few days before we left she started calling it Sweetheart. At the first gas station, Lisa ran around and opened the back of the truck. "Ready to come out?" she said. "Mommy will get you out now."

"How can you call yourself Mommy to a dog?" I said.

"Well, what other mother has she?"

Sometimes over at Lisa's, I used to fuss over the dog for a second, to make Lisa happy, but I don't remember it being any different from any other dog. It licked faces and sniffed crotches.

An hour later we were eating lunch at a rest stop. The dog was sitting there begging, its leash tied around Lisa's ankle. There were people sort of staggering from their cars to the restroom then back to their cars. Nobody was close to where they were trying to get that day. Lisa swallowed and said, "Anyway, Dexter, what else am I to her? I feed her, bathe her, clean up after her—"

But the dog wouldn't go to the bathroom. We gave it a chance every time we stopped for gas or to eat, but it never went. It must've been in such awful pain.

Lisa liked to check each riverbed as we went over it, looking over the side of the road and announcing how much water or if it was dry and what the name of it was. I can even remember some of them—Agua Fria, Clear Creek, Little Colorado, Puerco River, which means nasty or dirty. I asked her how would she like to go swimming in that one, then told her what it meant, but she didn't answer. She also didn't think it was funny that Beaver Creek was dry. Big crows sat on the highway picking at flat dry carcasses of possum or skunk, flying out of the way at the last possible moment, with Lisa sitting beside me muttering, "Go on, hurry, or you'll get squashed too and your friends and relatives'll be out here picking *you* apart." And she sat there worrying about her dog developing kidney problems from holding it in too long. But lots of time she sat there like nothing was bothering her at all.

At the border between California and Arizona, they have an inspection station. I had a box of tangerines in the back of the truck, but when they asked if I had any fresh produce or plants, I said no, and the inspector waved me through. After I'd gotten back up to 60 or 65 m.p.h., Lisa said, "Oh wow. I'm sweating. I'm shaking....Oh well, nothing to worry about, right?"

"What's the matter," I asked. "You okay?"

"We lied, that's all. We were able to lie so easily. Wow, I'm still sweating."

"You haven't had much practice lying, have you," I said.

"Not when it counts," she said, looking at me. She didn't usually look at me because she said she would get carsick if she didn't watch the road or the scenery. Sometimes she could glance down at a map, but not really long enough to find out much. That might be why she thought we could stop for the night in Steins, New Mexico.

There was only one exit into Steins, and at the bottom of the exit ramp it was too dark to see what anything looked like. No gas station, no cafe, no streetlamp. It was around 9:30, I guess. A sign said Steins was to the left, so we turned on a street that went back under the freeway, a tunnel so narrow I drove close to 5 m.p.h. because it looked like it might be easy to scrape up against the sides if you're not careful. The road was paved, but covered with rocks and other crap, so it felt like a dirt road. On the other side of the tunnel the road ended at a cross street, which was a *real* dirt road, and another small sign said that Steins was to the left again, but still no light in sight, nothing but black, then this big beam came from nowhere the same time we felt the underground thunder and Lisa let out a little scream. It was a train, seemed to be coming right toward us, but the track was just on the other side of the dirt road, swerved and went on past us, going east. Nothing would've stopped us from driving right onto the track, though, since we didn't know it was there, then this train comes out of nowhere, and no one around to see it happen. Lisa said it was like a Hitchcock movie. I said it was more like Mr. Toad's Wild Ride at Disneyland.

"That's the difference between us," she said.

"What?" I was back on the freeway by then.

She didn't answer at first, then, several miles later, said, "It's a relief to see a few other taillights ahead of us and some headlights going the other way, other people actually living a piece of their lives out here in the middle of nowhere the same time I am." I'd thought I knew her.

The next place east was Lordsburg, big enough for three freeway exits. We took the first one, to make sure we didn't miss what might be the cheapest motel in town, which happened to be the first one we got to, Molly's Motel, $15 for two people, one building, eight doors in a row, a muddy parking lot, an office with a 10-inch plastic Christmas tree lit with pink lights on the desk. They said they had one more room, but it didn't have a TV. Lisa said we didn't need a TV, but I got back into the truck and drove on anyway.

"Why aren't we staying there?" she asked.

"You didn't seem too happy about it."

"I didn't?"

They all looked alike. The next one was full. It was a U-shaped building with a mud parking lot and an empty swimming pool in the middle of the mud, more mud in the bottom of the pool. A slow train was going past on the track across the street. I said maybe it was the same train we'd seen in Steins. She was watching it too. There were other trains parked there, but it was so dark, all I could see was the one moving train going behind one that was standing still. There was a lot of clanking and hissing and huffing and puffing, but no human voice. The next motel was the Bel Aire and they had lots of room.

The bitch in the office was made-up for a night on the town, but didn't look up or smile. There was a sign on the desk that said "No Motorcycles In The Rooms!" I decided not to tell her about the dog that hadn't gone to the bathroom since we'd left San Diego that morning at six. She gave me some towels and I drove the truck down to where the room was. We were going to drop the bags into the room and take the dog for a walk right away, but we couldn't get the door to lock after we'd put our stuff inside. It just wasn't going to lock. The doorknob would lock and unlock, but either way, a shove on the door would open it. "I'm not staying here," Lisa said. She took the dog for a walk while I went back to the office to tell the clerk that the door didn't work. She wouldn't just take my word for it, had to come back to the room with me. It was freezing. I could see Lisa walking the dog in the mud in the dark parking lot, but no one knew we were together, so it could've been anyone as far as the clerk was concerned. I guess the train yard was big enough to be across the street from every motel in town. Another train was grinding to a halt.

She showed me how to lock the door, and I said I

knew how to lock it, but you could still push it open when it was supposedly locked. She said, "Sir, you're not listening, you have to turn this thing here to lock it."

"I know that, but it doesn't make any difference, the door opens anyway."

"Sir," she said, "I'm not going to argue with you, do you want me to show you how to lock it or not?"

"I know how to do it. Why don't you just give me another room." We were standing there in front of the door. All of a sudden there was a hiss and silence from the train yard across the street. God, it was cold. I could hear Lisa saying "Do your business" to the dog.

"All the rooms are the same, sir," the bitch said. "Do you want this room or your money back?"

"My money back."

She locked the door and closed it and was about to head back toward the office then stopped. "Where're the towels I gave you?"

"In the room," I said. She started to fumble around with the keys, but I said, "I'll get them," and shoved the locked door open with my shoulder, gave her a look, then went and got the dingy thin towels. Lisa was on her way back to the truck with the dog, the bitch was on her way to the motel office. I waited a second for Lisa, told her to get the dog out of sight, then ran up to the office. I had to come right back again for the receipt, though. Lisa was stuffing the dog into her travel cage, slammed the door, slammed the truck and whirled around. "Oh, it's only you," she panted.

In about an hour we were in a cafe eating Mexican food, the dog locked in the room we'd gotten at the

Holiday Motel, and I told Lisa the whole story about the bitch and the door. I acted out a few parts, like the whole conversation and the look I gave her. Lisa smiled a little, a little thin smile.

"You okay?" I asked. "Carsick?" I looked at the slop on my plate that was supposed to be a burrito. "Hell of a lousy place, huh?" I said. The waitress turned and grinned at me, then showed me this apron she was wearing that said, "Lordsburg Isn't The End Of The World. (But You Can See It From Here.)" I laughed. I'd heard it before in other places. Hungry Horse, Montana. Huachuca City, Arizona. But it's still funny. I told the waitress I was going to steal the slogan for a place in Arkansas I'd heard of called Toad Suck.

In the background the town know-it-all was having a conversation with a big guy in boots and a cowboy hat. The know-it-all was wearing some kind of uniform and had a CB radio on his belt which would crackle or pop every once in a while. He was telling the other guy how easy it is for people to sue schools or cities or even whole states. I caught Lisa's eye and sort of grimaced. She said, "At least we know no one in Lordsburg is hurt or sick."

"How d'we know that?"

"He's their paramedic. I saw his jeep out front."

"So that's good, then," I said, "no one's hurt or sick."

"No one that he knows of," she said. She hadn't eaten much. Mostly just her chips.

I said, "Except poor what's-er-name...Tracy."

"Yeah, poor old what's-er-name...."

The paramedic said, "Why d'ya think no one wants to build a park anymore? One kid slips on the jungle

80

gym and they sue for a million, and that's an out-of-court settlement."

"My divorce was an out-of-court settlement," I said. "And I didn't have to pay anything."

"You're divorced?" She looked up at me, holding her napkin like a rock in one fist.

"Didn't I tell you? Yeah, I told you. Didn't I?"

She didn't say anything else. The waitress closed the cafe right after we left. The mud in the parking lot was starting to freeze. A wind had come up and Lisa pressed against me a little until we got to our room. She slept all night with her back against my back, holding the dog in her arms. The trains never stopped groaning. I think Lisa was sleeping. In the morning she looked awful. I can only imagine how the dog felt, but it still wouldn't do anything when Lisa took it out. It was about 5:30. The windshield was frozen over so I was scraping it with a plastic spoon. Lisa had already stuffed the dog into her travel cage, but she hadn't gotten into the truck yet. She was standing in front of the door to our room. I said, "Hey!" and she looked at me. She had black bags under her eyes. "I already locked the room and turned the key back in." A train was pulling in or pulling out, I couldn't tell, it wasn't picking up any steam nor slowing down. It was still dark. We'd never actually seen what sounded and smelled like a jungle of trains fighting it out across the street. Lisa stepped in a frozen mud puddle on her way to the truck, slipped a little, then caught herself and swore under her breath. I laughed out loud.

"Shhh, Dexter, it isn't even six yet."

But I kept laughing, I don't know why. She was

81

getting hysterical, holding the antenna—I thought she was going to break it off—whispering and screaming at the same time, "Shut up, Dexter, shut up," her voice all raw and scraping, until she gave up the whisper and started screeching like the cold metal brakes on those trains, "Why didn't you tell me you got divorced!"

"For God's sake, Lisa...."

Before I could say much more she was squatting beside the front tire, moaning and crying, "I thought you'd be mad, I was afraid you'd be mad...."

Someone opened their door a crack, then closed it right away. "Mad at what?" I said.

"I thought you were still married, I didn't know, and now look where we are."

"Why're you making such a big deal out of everything, Lisa, it's just one night, and it's over now."

"One *night*? I'd've stayed here a thousand nights, what difference would it make where we lived, we could get a little house with a backyard for Tracy...a playground for the baby."

"Hey, I don't want any of that shit. Why'd'ya think I didn't say anything when you went and took care of it yourself?"

She screamed, "You *knew*?" She let herself fall backwards, put her butt right down in the cold mud. I wondered where that know-it-all paramedic was hiding when someone needed him.

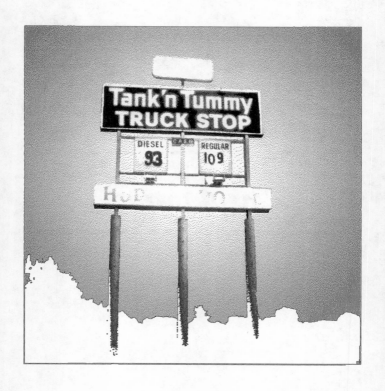

RECEDING MIRAGES

She wonders if it is always easier for a man...are they better equipped to face reality? Maybe Mark could've walked out the door, gotten into the car, driven away—just as she had to do—but would've immediately thought about other things: the next hotel garden he would design, new hybrid plants to use in dryer climates, a whitewater rafting trip he plans to take with his brother next year. He'll go on that trip, shout and laugh and get sunburned and tell true stories about it to friends (maybe also a woman), flipping plastic pages of a photo album. But *she* will never hear about that trip. Just as he will never hear about hers, this trip, now, heading west from Shreveport, staring straight ahead at the dark glossy wet spot on the freeway which always stays fifty yards ahead of her, evaporating before she gets there, reappearing farther away even as it dries under her wheels.

At three in the afternoon she's getting drowsy. In a rest stop, she hangs a sweater from the passenger window, puts a map over the driver's window and her cardboard sunshield over the dashboard, the huge

NEEDS ASSISTANCE letters pointed down at her body, folded sideways on the seat, her legs curled around her box of tapes. She dozes. The freeway thunder fades in and out, blurs with the sounds of people slamming doors; a groan from someone as he gets out of (or into) his car, kids shouting—looking for arrowheads in the gravel beds of the E-Z care landscaping. The noises swell enormously then dwindle to pinpricks, leaving only the sound of someone breathing. She smiles, sleeping, not sleeping, knowing it is Mark breathing, beside her, and in a moment he'll be the one moaning as he wakes, and he'll reach for her. The breathing is deep, a little rough, slow, close. Listening to his breath, she rises to consciousness, a child runs past her car, footsteps tapping quickly on the pavement, and she realizes before moving that it is her own breathing she hears.

In another hour she's getting gas at the Inland Island Last Stop—mini store, lunch-counter cafe, private showers for rent, one house trailer with a satellite dish, an incessant roar in the air from the freeway and from idling trucks. A large semi with a flat bed is loaded with three full-size palm trees, lying down, roots and all. The truck's license plate says California. She thinks about three big holes in the ground somewhere in California. The driver comes out of one of the shower doors, his hair slick, climbs into the cab and releases the air brake. The truck sighs, then jerks forward, rattling the tops of the trees which are tied to protect the fronds. The truck turns eastbound onto the freeway, an oasis on its way

to Oklahoma; she watches until the trees are out of
sight.

A few names of towns and cities given on freeway
signs stick in her mind: Wink, Hope, Star City, Loving,
Fate, Crump, Road Forks. And Sweetwater, where she
stops to eat a hamburger and hears two old coots
talking about the thunderstorm coming in. They have
to get home before it hits. *Why?* she wonders. What are
they so anxious about? They couldn't be worried about
memories coming to pound like a headache. They
probably have grapefruit trees to be concerned over, or
TV antennas, or birdhouses. Someday, when Mark
hears thunder trembling in the distance, will he think
of a night in Shreveport when they'd been the only
ones in the restaurant, the waiters outside pulling
cloths and candles off the patio tables as the wind
rattled the awning, crashed through the tree branches.
She and Mark sat clutching each other's hands, watching the light change to rosy black, waiting for the rain
to spatter suddenly against the window, losing their
heartbeats in the approaching thunder.

The storm had lasted until they were at his house,
and lasted after they went inside, and lasted until
morning, and she'd gone out the front door at 2:30 or
3 a.m., a shirt on but nothing else, the rain washed his
semen from her leg, the birds already singing although
it was still dark, without stars, the lightning still sparkling far off to the south. When she turned back to the
door, she thought, for a second, he'd gotten up and
locked her out—as a joke. But before she ever rattled the
door or called to him, the handle turned. The dampness
had made it stick. She'd returned to his dark bedroom,

wet, frisky, panting, and he was ready again.

Mark may not remember that night that way, may not remember a storm at all, might've teased her for embellishing. In that case, the thunderstorm in Sweetwater would be her first. She's driving toward it: the gentle sunset light turning ominous, rain like a waterfall against the glass, lightning snaking out of the sky, all branches and forks. But straight ahead it's raining light instead of water. That's where the lightning seems to come from, a thin part in the clouds, which becomes a hole in the clouds, a shower of light coming through, and two fingers of lightning at the same time, coming from that hole, one going left, one right, an arc over the freeway, a mile or so away, where she could've been if she'd left the hamburger stand when the old coots did. The lightnings exist only long enough to touch the ground somewhere. She can't hear the thunder over the sound of her engine. The hole in the clouds closes. On the frontage road beside the freeway, cars are parked under bridges. The rain thins. She accelerates from 40 to 50 then to 65. The clouds end up ahead, but the sun has gone down, so she never is allowed to suddenly burst through the end of the storm and into the light which she had been able to see up ahead for so many miles.

She isn't ready to wake up and start driving again. Someone outside has lost Steve. A car door slams and footsteps crunch, then rapping on the motel room door next to hers. "Steve?" a woman calls. No answer.

"Steve!" She pounds on the door. She is using her knuckles, knocking, then her fist. "Steve!" She walks away a few steps, comes back, kicks the door or uses her knee. "Steve, open the door!" She taps, she knocks, she thumps, she may be using her forehead. "Steve!" There is still no answer and the woman leaves. A car door thuds and someone drives away. Another door opens and a dog barks. Suddenly the woman is back, knocking, banging, calling "Steve!" Steve is a heavy sleeper. Or he doesn't want to answer the door. Or he is dead. Or he isn't in there at all. Will Steve ever realize a woman pounded on his door at five in the morning, calling his name, letting everyone know she'd lost him?

It is after the woman has given up on Steve that a man almost loses Coal. Coal has run away. She can tell because the man isn't knocking on a door. He's shouting, "Coal, come!" Where is Coal—in the strip of garden in front of the Arby's next door? Sniffing around the dumpsters? Cornering a stray cat under a motorhome? The man calls, "Coal, get back here!" She never hears a jingle of tags nor the rough panting of a happy roaming dog, but Coal must've come back because finally the man is saying, "You'd better behave or I'll kick your ass." It still isn't time to get up and start driving again.

Something on the horizon, a ranch gate or tree or tower, isn't getting any closer. But she *is* approaching then passing other things. Mostly signs. Possibly the same signs as yesterday, giving names of truck stops she'll maybe never get to, motels that might not exist— but there are signs that say so, over and over, as though she's been driving in a circle so huge she can't feel the curve of it. She's been having her period, mostly spotting, for three weeks now. The pads have chaffed her skin, there's a damp rash. She pushes her hips forward in the seat, unzips her pants, rips out the mini pad. She's been sweating so the blood is diluted to pale pink. No cars are close behind. She opens the window a crack and flips the pad out onto the freeway. Then she has to watch—will a flashing Texas state trooper bear down on her, force her to the side of the road, then approach her car holding the pad in two fingers at eye level when she rolls down her window?

She might've wanted to stop and see, even touch, the totem pole with a wolf's head on top, advertised on yellow signs every half mile—it's standing just about where the freeway veers a little to the left. But when she finally feels it necessary to turn the wheel (so slightly it's as though she only has to *think* about turning), the totem pole isn't there. Unless it's the tall thing still on the horizon which doesn't get any closer, slinking away from her. A radio transmitter? Telephone pole? A hitchhiker with suitcases around his feet? She passes a pile of trash bags left by the road department to be picked up later. When she turns to glance at the bags, it's almost as though she's sitting still while they are moving east away from her, backing up and vanishing. But the hitchhiker who seemed to be standing beside the bags is still far up ahead, also disappearing.

"It's just a mirage," she says out loud when the

hitchhiker appears again, one arm jaggedly stuck out like the limb of an old tree, not getting any bigger nor closer—retreating, then dissolving once more. A shattered STUCKY'S sign in an abandoned parking lot looms in front suddenly, slips past and begins its gentle descent toward the east: *It's* not a mirage, just looks the same. Anything that drifts away, quietly, easily, serenely, while you speed *toward* it—70, 75, 80 m.p.h.—it isn't there in the first place. The things that disappear *behind* you (just as placidly) were really there. As long as the road barely turns, she can stay in her lane while looking behind herself—why not just use the rear view mirror instead of the front windshield?

Every time she passes anything big enough to notice—a fencepost with a WARNING posted, a freeway road marker, signs for the same motels she'll never see—she watches them dwindle away behind her, like small figures falling from a skyscraper, spinning and dropping out of sight. She's sure the hitchhiker is right under the road sign giving the mileage to El Paso and Las Cruces. The sign gets clearer, easier to read, but when it skims over the top of the car, there's no hitchhiker, suddenly human, on the side of the road. He's still far up there where the road narrows to a point, never gets nearer, continues to fade away or retreat out of sight. Maybe it's Steve and this is why the woman at the motel could pound on the door until her fist or head splintered through, but no Steve would ever answer. He was hitchhiking all along, but no one would ever stop for him because no one could get to him. And he might not even mind. Like someone in a film who can never be touched—and if you look hard enough you can see the texture of the screen in his skin. The horizon unwinds like a movie projected on the low sky in front of her. She glances into the rear view mirror to watch the back of the mileage sign swirl out of sight—grips the steering wheel so tightly her nails gouge her palm. *The hitchhiker is also behind her.* She can clearly see his maroon backpack, black baseball cap on his head, canvas jungle boots, a red plaid flannel shirt flapping in the breeze made by cars that whip past. The sun is directly overhead—there are no shadows anywhere. The hitchhiker behind her moves away from her as though on a slow conveyer belt—much slower than it takes the signs and lone trees to disappear. He withdraws tranquilly into the distant haze just like the same hitchhiker who is still in front of her. The horizon behind actually looks exactly like the horizon in front: both receding, both rolling away. As though she's on a mountain which is shooting swiftly higher into the sky, with her on the point, holding on, the world stretching out bigger and bigger and farther away. If the hitchhiker who's always in front is a mirage, is the one (*still* visible) behind her not real either? Are his canvas boots and black hat not real? Is his maroon pack not real? His red shirt? Can she really still see his eyes in the mirror as she puts a mile between them every minute, his eyes watching her go without expression, without a question, without a glint of tears, getting smaller and smaller, but still familiar enough to be someone she knows...or has known...or the Steve she's never met. She says out loud, "It's all been a mirage."

Her eyes vibrate and lose focus, the steering wheel jumps out of her hands, her foot bounces off the gas, a spray of rocks crashes against the underside of the car, her head hits the ceiling and knocks the rear view mirror askew, wood crunches, she can't find the pedals, doesn't know where to look, how could she suddenly be driving off the road if just a second ago she was watching the horizon and the freeway feeding into it?

The car stands still, finally, tipping slightly to one side, on a wide, bumpy shoulder of the road, the weeds growing as high as her windows. She cuts the motor and closes her eyes. Listens to herself breathe. Louder than the sound of the cars still moving east to west on the freeway beside her. It *is* her own breathing—there's no hitchhiker who'll be peering at her through the window when she opens her eyes. No Steve who'll finally answer the woman's desperate call, "Who, *me*?" And no Mark whose eyes will still be saying, *It's been fun, goodbye, have a good life.*

When she does open her eyes, the two horizons are still identical. No hitchhiker in sight either way. The sky hazy white behind low fuzzy and faintly purple swells of land. Two horizons, but, now, neither moving away. A sign in the west announces a single room for $20. A sign in the east says free cable TV and phones. She unfolds her sunshield like an accordion with both hands. On one side the customary gigantic pair of sunglasses. A spot on the freeway a quarter mile to the west looks wet, and another spot to the east is also wet, but she doesn't know if it rained recently. The wet spots shimmer. She lets the cardboard sunglasses stare *into* the car, from the back windshield, and the other side of the shield faces out, the big red letters: NEEDS ASSISTANCE.

93

❖

While she sleeps, the wind makes a dry weed scratch against the car, which drifts in and out of her hearing until it gets louder and more persistent, knocking on her window, saying "Hey lady," and she opens her eyes. It's a man with stylish long hair, short on the sides, an earring in his left ear—a green gem which catches the sun. He's wearing a T-shirt with a tuxedo painted on the front, including a red carnation at the lapel and a pleated shirt. When she opens the door, he steps back; his feet—at the bottom of his faded jeans, nearly lost in the scrubby weeds—are in rubber thongs.

"Are you a hitchhiker?" she asks, sliding out of the car to stand facing him.

"I saw your sign. I can give you a lift to a phone or something."

"Were you hitching?"

"Lady, I've got a truck, do you speak English? *I* can give *you* a ride."

His truck is parked behind her. Not a decently huge 18-wheeler which never makes anyone doubt its existence (with a silver profile of a naked woman on its rear tire flaps), but an ancient, white-and-rust, paint-peeling small panel truck with a dim red hen on the side and black script letters: BRADY'S EGG FARM.

"Is your name Steve?" she asks.

He runs his slim fingers through his hair. "Did you have an accident? Bump your head or something?"

"I stopped for a hitchhiker."

"You crazy? I don't stop for *no*body out here. Gotta be careful. Were you robbed or something? Did he attack you?"

"I don't think so. I was transferred to Phoenix, so I have to move there. I just had to leave. One morning it was my last day so I had to go, what else could I do?" She feels blood trickle on the inside of her thigh, grasps the crotch of her pants.

The man takes a step back. "Lady, what planet did you come from?"

She laughs, closes her eyes. "A planet...yes, a goddamn star...Shreveport. Was only there a month. Not even a hole in the ground where my roots were. Now Phoenix...." With one hand she reaches in her pants, still unzipped, to scratch the rash. Her other hand is suddenly groping for him, her arm swinging in a wide arc because her eyes are still closed and she doesn't know exactly where he is—still, as expected, she touches nothing. But hears his voice say, "Knock it off, Lady, you for real? What're ya tryna do?"

"I don't *hafta* be careful, Steve," she says. "I'm out here in the middle of nowhere, my hand passing right through you, my other hand all bloody, talking to myself, aren't I?" She reaches out again, swinging her arm, feels her hand brush the tops of the tallest grasses— then, almost the instant her breath catches as she touches his shirt, she is hit, her arm is stopped, struck down in mid-swing, sending her backwards into the weeds. Her eyes bounce open as her ass hits the ground. The man is walking away from her, quickly, back to his truck, his footsteps and the crunching weeds sound too loud, until her own voice blares out: "Wait!"

His, coming from farther away now, is tinny and distant: "I knew I shouldn't'a stopped for no one out

95

here, but your car looked *normal."*

"Wait, I *am* normal!" She gets up and tries to run after him, the bumpy ground jarring her head so much she can't see where she's going. She has to watch her feet. It seems she has to run forever, for miles, but can't get closer. She hears the truck door slam, sticks crack beneath her feet, rocks roll away as she steps on them— she lurches sideways, keeps her balance, then crashes against the door of his truck which she'd thought was still so far away she'd never get there before he started backing up, speeding up, putting even more distance between them. She slaps his window with her palms. One hand has blood under the nails. "Please, take me to a phone, I have to make a call."

He starts the engine.

"Please!"

He guns the motor, staring straight ahead. She smacks the window again. "Okay." His voice is muffled inside the car. He turns to where her palms are pressed against the glass. "Okay, but go get in back, I'm not letting you up here with me."

She pulls her hands away, feeling they were almost stuck there like suction cups. The back of the egg truck is nearly empty, a few wire crates, a blanket in the corner. It reeks of musk cologne. What a mirage smells like, she thinks, feeling the truck accelerate. She hears the asphalt under the tires when he pulls onto the freeway, then can tell when he down-shifts to take an exit. When he stops, he thumps on the back wall of the truck's cab, so she gets out.

The sign over the souvenir store and gas station says OASIS TRAVEL STOP, the words in a rainbow shape hovering over a seemingly life-size concrete palm tree, outlined in neon. The green leaves have been bleached to a sickly yellow, the brown trunk faded to lilac. At that moment she and the egg truck man are moving in opposite directions: him toward the buildings while she runs to a phone booth, standing alone at the other end of the parking lot, where she gasps "Shreveport" when the operator asks what city. The operator says, "What number do you want...hello? What number, please. Hello?"

From the glass booth, she watches the man come back from the other side of the store, zipping his pants. His truck is the only one in the lot. Weeds have squeezed through cracks in the pavement. She can hear flies buzzing. The operator says, "What name in Shreveport, please." He locks the back of his truck. She watches him get into the front seat, fasten his seatbelt, release the brake and begin moving the truck back toward the freeway without ever using his rear view mirror.

"Did you want to be connected?" the operator says.

"Uh...Mark...?" her voice trailing away, like words thrown from a passing car, while she drops the receiver which hangs from its cord and swings slowly back and forth, as though abandoned long ago.

ON THE CIRCUIT

You know I didn't want to go, but you said this circuit came at exactly the right time...so we could each think about some things. I tried to explain what happened, what you saw. Maybe you'll listen when I get back. Maybe I'll explain it better. I love you. Isn't that enough? Apparently not. As far as Katie goes...to think, you and I wouldn't have even met if Katie hadn't finally gotten the position she wanted training sea lions at the zoo. I could've predicted it—I've known her for 8 years. I've seen it happen dozens of times. But when she wants a man, know what kind of man she likes? Not men— boys. Smooth, hairless, fresh-scrubbed, red-lipped boys. You had too many lines on your face from the African sun. Too many scars, too much experience on your skin. Your nose and ears frozen a few too many times while counting penguins in Antarctica. Too many things your eyes have seen—squinting against wind or glare, or pressed to binoculars—which faded the color, used up the vivid green or blue. Yet for all you've seen and done and heard all over the world, you still thought there was something for you behind her glossy smile, her clean straw-colored hair, her laughing eyes. Jay, she would've culled you out like a deformed puppy, only worse, botched it, left you half alive in the toilet, gurgling through a split palate. What would you've done if I hadn't been there to fish you out? Let's forget it. Why do we have to keep remembering, it doesn't have to stay around in our heads forever like bad perfume, making my eyes water.

I smell sulphur. I hope there's not something wrong with the engine. Pumping out poison gas all this time, killing all the animals in the back, and just now working its way up to me. Oh, there's some sort of factory out there. Maybe that's it.

Why can't I call you? I told you I'd cancel the circuit, send all these dogs back to their owners, but maybe you think it's more important for me to see Virginia and Maryland in the fall. Big deal, leaves change colors. You're a beautiful color, but you won't let me say it. Sunset colored, like this mahogany Sheltie bitch I'm showing now. I went out with a black man once, football player, more charcoal than red/brown like you, smooth and cool and charcoal and smelled like musk cologne. Certain department stores, I think of him. Nothing to remind me of you…a smell all your own. You didn't like that either, I know, and said, "People aren't supposed to smell." Of course we do, how'd'ya think my dog does the scent discrimination exercise, anyway? What's there to think about, Jay? Why can't I call you tonight? I miss you, it's been a week.

Cows outside. Grassy animal smell. Just now unrolled my window so I could hear the cowbells like you described it in Switzerland, the miles of silence and tinkling cowbells, far and near, like wind chimes in the Alps, a cold and pristine tone, a sound that spreads you out so you're everywhere at once, out in the pasture, floating on the sprinkled glitter of cowbells. I heard it when you described it to me. I hear nothing here but the rubber conveyer-belt noise of my fat wheels on the road, rip of wind past the window, trucks in front of and behind me. It's funny, you travel all over the world to write your wildlife books and make your nature documentaries. I travel all over the country showing dogs of manipulated, man-made, genetically troubled breeds, collecting championship points for this sterile surgery-improved stud, or that allergy-ridden, skin-syndrome carrier bitch. What can I share with or describe to you that's anywhere near the sound of lions breathing just beyond the light of your fire, monkeys screaming at dawn, walruses crashing tusks....The sound of a dog show? A pen of yapping Yorkies just outside the motorhome window. A fat woman yammering about getting dumped in the specials class while she trims a terrier and says, "Dammit, stand still, Striker, or I'll poke your eye out." The constant churn of motorhome generators. The loud speaker calling for a janitor to ring 4. The tinny national anthem at 8 a.m. Floating lingo: cuts size...coat factor...natural ears...he put up that ugly bitch...is the AOC class in yet?...doggy-bitch ...needs socializing...won't show...he knows there's a bitch in season around here...I was dumped...I had a good go but he didn't really dig in and work for me...wrong handler on the end of the leash. Barking and howling and scattered applause and screams of the point-winners and the crash of pens being collapsed, grooming boxes slammed, crying children slapped.

Now I smell natural gas. Is my stove leaking back there? Would a burning engine smell like natural gas? God, that's the type of foolish girl-question Katie asks you, isn't it, in a sing-song high voice, a different voice than when she told me, more than once, how if you tried to touch her with your huge scaly hands she'd run away screaming. She said it touching my arm. I just stared at her. I just shrugged. But I hated you for being so stupid. I hated you most of all the day Katie and I went shopping for her camera, and you showed up— did she coyly ask for help or did you gallantly offer?— with your splendid hazy far-away eyes and your lovely gentle hands on the glass-topped display counter. You looked through to the cameras and lenses, I looked at your hands spread on the glass and felt sick to my stomach because I knew I knew I knew...that I didn't hate you at all. Losing always seems more real, so I didn't ever bother to wonder if you would stop looking at your hands and touching your face with distaste because she was repulsed...or eventually smile because I called you beautiful. It all worked out for the best, though, you said. We found each other. A miracle that you ever met my eyes. But how many times did I have to hear about her amazing intuitive talent with the sea lions, the depth of her knowledge of animal behavior, her fascinating experience training dolphins and birds and wild cats. Maybe that's all I was doing with her that night, trying to find even the faintest glimpse or scent of what you saw. Maybe trying to find out if I had it too. Because if I do, whatever it is, I'd show it to you, give it

102

to you. You never even came to one dog show. I'm the only professional handler I know of who shows in both breed and obedience, but you said, "What kind of person has to use their housepet for meaningless cut-throat competition?" You thought I should use my experience with dogs to study wild canine packs, get a government grant for research, travel with you to Africa or Asia. Don't think for a second, Jay, that it doesn't sound wonderful...all the things you've de-scribed to me, with my eyes shut and heart open, your voice packed with fervent energy, giving me 100 times more than your pictures or books could hope to express...I could feel the hot cloud of dust, smell the animal musk as your open jeep bumped along in the middle of a seemingly infinite herd of wildebeest, my body tensed with adrenalin as you rode in a bus tipping almost sideways around turns on ledges in Brazil, tasted the odor of sweat and rotting garbage when you shared a first-class train compartment with a humming Hindu in India all afternoon while the train baked in the sun and went nowhere. Or in Papua, New Guinea, one of my favorite places I've never been, when you could only get around by helicopter, you and a chopper pilot, looking for lizard specimens in a place where there are undiscovered tribes of people, maybe 400 or more, each with its own territory and language, constantly war-ring, killing easily, life is cheap...if they don't get killed by each other, disease eats them alive. You two guys needing permission as you crossed from one territory to the next, having to befriend each tribe you came to, "don't offend," the pilot told you at the banquet, "eat what they give you." It was hard, black, fried, tough, gamey and strong...it was whole bats. Then the gifts had to be exchanged. Death for not accepting a gift. And gifts had to be given in return—a bigger better gift. When they gave you a bone necklace, you gave it back and added empty film containers. When they gave you a spear, you gave it back and added a canteen. When they gave you a woman—with three teeth and flies in her eyes—you gave her back and added a leather belt. But pigs are valued above women. Pigs, the ultimate gift, couldn't be given back. No gift was greater. You took the pig in your arms, the vermin visible on its skin, under the caked manure and bristly hairs, its slimy nose against your neck, its shriek of fright in your ears as the chopper took off, swung over a low hill half a mile away and landed again so the still squealing pig could be let loose in the brush.

After that, what kind of travel story can I share with you? Maybe the rest stop in California on the local circuit last month where I stopped to call you—more like a street fair than travel area, people selling home-made jewelry from blankets spread on the sidewalk, loud radios, laughter, an ice cream vendor. Or watching the local news in Boise, they had a cooking segment...probably done on the news 5 days a week, 52 weeks a year, but when I was there one night in my life, turned it on and they were doing: how to bake a potato. Or how about the retirement city in Nevada, spread out along the freeway, a Buick dealer who only has big white sedans with grey/blue crushed velvet interiors next door to a Kentucky Fried Chicken next door to a mortuary. And out in the desert, 20 miles from the closest gas station, the huge sign that says "Future

Home of Johnson Brothers Piano and Organ Supermarket." Oh, a judge told a good breakdown story in the motel lounge the other night, about ten of us sitting around. In the proverbial middle-of-nowhere his car limps to a clunking, wheezing halt on the side of the road. It's his axle. It's broken. The closest place is a truck stop, 100 miles away, called Little America. Biggest truck stop in the world. Puts out his Needs Assistance sign. No response. An hour goes by. He's got his wife and child along on this particular judging assignment. Places her strategically beside the car holding the baby to prove he's normal and really needs help. He's got the broken axle in his hand. Finally a trucker takes him. He leaves his wife and child locked in the car. But nobody at Little America can help him—they only have truck parts. Also showers, motel rooms, five-thousand souvenirs, travel comfort novelties, plaid jackets, gloves, sunglasses, bottle openers, gold rings, camouflage hunting coveralls, boots, condoms, deodorant, just-add-water chicken soup, ice scrapers, toilet paper, bathing suits, hundreds of kinds of cookies, a video arcade, truck wash, the longest lunch counter in the world and dozens of leatherette booths with a phone at every one…but no axles. He'll need a lift to the nearest town. Stands at the edge of the truck stop, holding up the axle, waving at each car, holding the axle higher so they'll know he really needs help, isn't an escaped convict or deranged car thief, but a dog show judge who's also a college professor during the week. Finally he starts shouting as each car passes him, "Hey, I'm a Shakespeare teacher!" Holding up that axle, grease running down his arm. I said, "Alas poor Yorick, I knew him," and the judge smiled at me. Maybe that's why he and I ended up in his suite, me on the table like a 3-course-dinner, he dug away at me, pushing my knees up and back like turning an orange section inside out so you can scrape all the fruit from the rind. I took the breed under him with a fox terrier bitch the next day.

What's that stink...something rotting, something dying or already dead a long time. Sometimes cats crawl into the engine area from underneath, because it's warm—then get chewed to pulp and grease the engine up good the next time I start driving. No, I think there's a paper mill somewhere around here.

It's quiet without Queenie whining back there. She was bred this morning before we left the show grounds. That's why I'm a little late. She wanted to play around, flirt, get her ears licked, wag her ass at him and dance. He kept leaving to go pee...had nothing to pee on except the sides of the exercise pen. Finally we had to hold her and cut out the nonsense, so he could do his job. Then the goddamn tie lasted 20 minutes. Well, at least they took the bitch for the next two or three breedings so I won't have to deal with it anymore. Maybe it used to be sort of fun, almost like a party for everyone around, but somehow, after a thousand times, it's lost its charm.

But remember those giraffes at the zoo? You didn't even need to give me one of your behind-the-scenes tours. That stud giraffe with his 2-foot rod, following the girl around, his head bobbing and nodding with the same rhythm as his plodding rhythmic feet and his wagging black cock, always dripping a little from the end, too. They would cross necks and side-step in a circle, he'd rear up to mount her but she'd already be walking away, her head nodding too, her eyes as big and dreamy as his, lids half closed. Kids in the crowd asked what they were doing.

"Playing, honey."

"Dancing."

"They love each other."

I still don't know why you wouldn't hold my hand. Stood there leaning your forearms on the rail, your after-lunch drowsy eyes blinking slowly. I wanted to stand behind you and wrap my arms around you, put my chin over your shoulder.

She didn't want to stand for him. I didn't think anything would happen. Just the same rhythmic, nodding circle, crossed necks, tails swishing back and forth. She kept walking, kept walking, and as long as she kept walking, nothing would be completed. If they wanted a baby giraffe at the zoo, I told you, someone would have to hold her still. But suddenly she braced all four legs and he mounted her. It was like he could control the direction and angle of his long black cock with some muscle somewhere. It arced up toward under her tail and penetrated, but just the tip, just a couple of inches, and just for a second. Then they parted, walked opposite directions, and he pulled his rod back in, the last string of drool that had been coming out of it sort of broke off and hit the dust. All that play, but that's all he wanted.

The crowd dispersed but we stayed. One of those winter days in California where the sun is like a warm bath. We sat on a peanut-shaped bench, then I stretched out full length, my head on your leg. You took the end of my hair and brushed my forehead with it like a paintbrush. You were going to New Zealand for 2 months the next day. That night, when we still hadn't spoken since the zoo, that was when we looked at each other in the spotted light of dusk—a time your eyes are usually black holes, but this once I saw them shining, languid but keen—and I slowly rolled over, stood on elbows and knees while you gripped me by the waist and slid into me...deep, forever, as though there was no end to anything or either of us...you lay your chest along my back, your teeth and breath damp on my shoulder blade, you were wired and powerful, and the tiny kiss on my neck tenderly pushed me into spasms.

Were either of us thinking of Katie? I don't think so. Did you know it was my first time that way? And I loved it. Loved it. You should know that. You think anything else can send me places like you do? You think anything can tingle like the rush I get just seeing your grey eyes close and your teeth biting your lower lip as you come and then collapse against me, or taste as sweet as the sweat on your neck, or push me as powerfully as your velvet moan in my ear? Not even my elusive someday Best-in-Show will make me as proud as when you say you're thinking of me while filming seals off Galapagos Island, or when you softly touch my back at a fund-raising cocktail party, or when you smile at me across the crowd at one of your book-signings. You think anything else measures up? No, and especially not that pathetic light tapping I hear at night on my motorhome, which I'm never sure is real until I open the door, which I never do unless I'm alone, which I always am until I hear the first light knock. Sometimes it might be a judge who might take an extra look at the dog on my lead if he sees me in the ring the next day; more often another handler who'll crowd me, block the judge's view of me, distract my dog, break its stack as the judge comes down the row. I should tell you about this, so you'd know that Katie meant nothing to me, meant no more than any of them. If I'm not with someone I cry at night. God, I'm so hungry I'm nauseous...and can smell bread baking. Like driving into a doughy, yeasty fog-bank. That surely couldn't be something wrong with my engine.

I have to know, Jay—would you have asked Katie to join us for lunch at the zoo employees' cafeteria that day if she didn't invite herself first? You're the one who answered yeah, sure, pull up a chair, before I could barely raise my eyes. Yes, she's been my friend for eight years—and I probably did expect to see her in there, at least I wasn't surprised—but girls should know when to leave each other alone. Did I say anything else the rest of the lunch? I can only remember what she said. "Are you having the nachos again, Jay? I thought they made you sick last time. Oh, thanks again for helping me get that old sofa to the dump. I've almost decided on my color scheme—what do you think of tan and white? Did you say a money market was better than a CD account? I should've brought your videotape back— that was a great show, thanks." Yes, I heard your voice answering her. I stared at your hand on the table. I touched your leg with my knee to see if you would move away. You didn't. What, you might ask me now, would I have done if you did move your leg away? But, Jay, it seems I have no answers. Maybe you gave me the idea when you squeezed my shoulder and said, "See you later," then "You too, Katie" to her. But I don't think I had an idea. I don't remember. She smiled up at you as you left, and then at me. Was I drunk? you asked that night. Was I stoned? I probably was acting like it when I just lay there staring at you while she threw her clothes on and tore out of there. If you hadn't been pulling the sheet up over me while you asked, "Is this something about you two I didn't know about?" I might not've said, "Just something about *her* you didn't know about. Imagine that, something about Katie you managed not to know." While you walked around my bed, looking at the photos on the wall—your photos, lions chewing on skeletal carcasses, zebras drinking from their own reflections, a tree leaved in white birds—know what I wanted you to do? I wanted you to hold me like I'd been mugged or raped or thrown from a speeding car and you'd found me in a gutter. But all that had happened, Jay, was she licked at me like a kitten. No more than that. No more than when I drop my hand over the side of the bed and whatever dog is there licks it, carefully between each finger, slowly across the palm, while I think about the judges on my next circuit, an ad I'm planning for *The Pacesetter*, the cookies I put in the freezer, or what I'll say or do for you when you come home from Africa or Australia or Alaska that'll make you know how I love you.

Now you'll probably never believe it. But you've probably never seen two bitches in standing heat, side by side, flagging for each other, each looking over her shoulder at the other. They feel their own hunger and smell the other's. Maybe we all turn too much into dogs while on a circuit. It's no different. We feel that tug in our guts when we make eye contact, we crave, we scent, we hunger, we want to lick each other's lips and ears and stare each other down and wag our asses to invite play and bare our teeth when enough's enough. But that's not what love is. Do you think that's what love is to me? Don't think it. If it were, then it would be true...I'd have nothing to offer you that you can't get anywhere, anywhere, from anyone, anyone anywhere.

BMW CONVERSATION

You know, I never thought I'd be caught dead in a car like this, I mean—

Why?

Because of...you know ...money, power, Republicans, the kind of thing I—

You just wait. This car would make Republicans pee in their pants. Your liberals too. Without regard to race, politics or social classes. You sure you want to do this?

Yes! I want a ride like there's no tomorrow. Will it be scary?

It's not scary—sensational, powerful, nothing else can make you feel so pumped.

That's what I mean by scary. I want you to go real fast!

Fast doesn't begin to describe what I'm going to do. You have no idea—you haven't lived until you feel what this car can do.

Oh boy! Can you guarantee I won't die?

I mean on this trip, will I be killed?

No. You'll die.

It's perfectly safe. I know what I'm doing. Everything's under control.

But what if I grab your arm while we're speeding around a curve...and... okay, I throw you off balance and we go careening into a bumpy cow field and...you know...and flip end-over-end twenty times ...and then...and then... and land upright so we go zooming forward again straight into the side of a horse barn so the horses all get let loose and stampede—

114

Then don't grab my arm. Ready? Here we go!

Oh my *god*...Oh god....

This is a real fun place, it's great because the corners are tricky, but there aren't any driveways or other streets to worry about.

God...it's like riding a roller coaster, but *my* seat's on a *rocket*...and it's not even *attached* to the track... oh...my god....

We don't need to be attached. I know right where to put the wheels at the apex of the corner, just slide the back-end a little that way, we'll hit 140 on the straightaway.

Oh god, oh god, oh god...I hope I'm not putting fist-prints in your expensive upholstery...no, wait...oh, wait—

It's not really as dangerous or daring as it seems. Trust me, I always know exactly how the car will respond.

I believe you...but I didn't know...*god*...it's like...I can't tell whether I'm tied in a knot or my whole body's just a melted wet spot on the seat....

Just relax, everything's okay. You'll see, I know what I'm doing. See, here I'll have to accelerate hard in 3rd—we're going about 100—a quick change to 4th, RPM's rising, then this high-speed right-hander, still accelerating, look: 130.

Right up here, there's this series of esses. I have to keep the car finely balanced, still in 4th, flick of the wrist to the left, hard on the loud pedal, then right then left again, through the esses—this car hauls ass through esses.

Wow, I—

Okay, I have to brake hard here, an easy left-hander, uphill, into 2nd, a constant radius, dual apex right-hander—accelerate hard through it, upshift to 3rd,

I can't see straight...my eyeballs are rattling... oh...oh god....

116

to 4th for this undulating quarter-mile straightaway.

Jesus Christ...I don't...I can't....

But now we're coming to an uphill ninety-degree left-hander—brake hard at the last second, off the loud pedal, back on quickly, accelerate through this sweeping right-hander. Look, see how the road gets wider—I let the car drift all the way almost into the marbles on the left side, there's a nice long straightaway ahead, I'll go through all the gears, almost redlining in 4th, but, see, not enough room to get into 5th.

Oh no...why is it...I mean ...oh no....

Now a sweeping long slightly banked right-hander with a very late apex, so I have to do a quick heel-and-toe, back down to 3rd, accelerate gradually around, little by little letting the car feed in, ever so slowly, to hit the late apex. I can feel I'm at the limit of adhesion, the left front tire getting very hot. But now I'm finally going to hit this apex, nail the throttle and let the car come all the way out, using every available inch.

What's wrong?

It's okay, don't worry, here's some air. Lots of people get sick, don't be embarrassed.

Here? Where're you going to lie down?

There's no shoulder, just sand, you don't want to get out here, just a sec., there's a few cross streets up ahead, there'll probably be a Burger King or some-

Oh...oh...help...no, wait, I—

It's...I...it's...I don't feel so good.

Stop, I have to get out and lie down.

Outside. Anywhere. The smell of leather and air-conditioner is making me nauseous.

thing. It might be the last chance to eat for a while.

Eat! I don't wanna eat. I'll just lie down on the grass outside. Jeez, incredible, I thought the only danger would be crashing.

And then having to explain why you were in my car.

You could crash well enough so we wouldn't have to worry about it...let them worry after we're dead. Let them wonder. Or maybe you could crash so well they'd never even know it was 2 people.

But it had 2 heads.

I wish I didn't have a head right now. Or a stomach.

We're almost there. I'm going real slow. More air? I can open the sunroof.

A sunroof...it's even got a goddamn sunroof....

You gonna be sick right now? I can stop. Don't be embarrassed. It even happens to professional race drivers. I heard of an instructor who took a student around a track—when they stopped, the instructor got out and was sick all over.

I just wanna lie down.

After we eat, if you still want to go on, you can drive, would that help?

You'd trust me with this thing?

Sure. It's easy. You'll love how it feels. Like you can do *any*thing.

If you were going around these curves real fast, would you ever have just 2 wheels on the road?

No, that would be out of control. I want to have as much of that rubber surface on the road as possible. A corner can be done just as fast with all four tires on the pavement.

But if the police catch you, your ticket would say something about reckless driving. Funny, huh?

If just anybody did it, it *would* be reckless.

Maybe I'm feeling better ...no, I don't know....

C'mon, I'll get you a milkshake, that'll help.

Maybe...oh god, maybe not. God, a milkshake—sometimes we sound like we're in junior high. Can I lie down on the floor in Burger King? Wow, take it easy on the turns.

I'm going 25 miles an hour in a parking lot! It's okay, see, I'm parking now, we're stopped, not moving at all. Okay? Don't be embarrassed.

I'll be right back.

Just go ahead, I'll wait here.

❖

Oh—are you going to drive now? Sure you don't want any of this milkshake?

No thanks. How far is it to the top of the mountain?

Are we still going up there?

We're not quitting just because my stomach's upset.

You can stop as many times as you need.

Damn right! I'm sure sorry
I feel this way.

Hey, don't apologize. It's
okay. I mean, I don't want
you to feel sick, but it
hasn't ruined my day. I
don't mean that like it
sounds...it *sounds* like a
crummy thing to say. What
the hell do I mean?
Well...*you* know what I
mean, don't you?

Yes. *I* just mean, damn,
damn, *damn*, I didn't want
to feel this way. God, this
is a twisty road. When I'm
with you, I should feel
nothing but fabulous. But,
hey, it doesn't change anything. It's still a perfect
day. And it *was* a great ride.
What a rush!

It's funny...considering
what this car was built
for...aren't you taking
these corners at about 20
miles an hour...? I can't
see the gauge—

Yeah, I wanted to run
amok today, do something
fast and insane.

Maybe later you'll feel better...? I could—

Oh god, I'm stopping. Right here. I don't care what the signs say.

Okay, okay—

Better? This is a dangerous place...that's a blind corner and someone could—

How dangerous could it be? At least I can see straight for a second. At least the line down the center of the road isn't rippling like a snake in front of me. It's no more dangerous than sitting in my living room. Someone could've come up the street and crashed through my front window, and we'd've been found there sitting in two chairs, not even our hands touching.

And never know how good we could've been together.

That's not—

I know.

My timing must just stink, is that it?

Mine does too.

I don't have to go out and purposely do anything crazy: I'm excited all day because a man who's not even my lover will come spend an hour or two with me in the afternoon. Insane.

I know. But it's the same for me, I—

I'm ready to go again, let's go. You know, I always thought these cars were ugly, the kind of car where you'd be sure to find a baby seat in the back.

No baby seats here.

But that's not the only thing that makes a car ugly.

Okay, most of 'em *are* ugly, like boxes. But they're not all the same—

Neither are the owners.

What do you mean?

You know, young businessmen, financial guys, they get their MBA and their BMW, their long-sleeved white shirts and ties flapping over their shoulders, plans for something rolled-up under one arm, one foot in a loafer propped on a desk chair while they point at a computer screen, make reports, call in on car phones, fax documents, give presentations, all that stuff they do....

Is that a long, back-handed compliment?

You know damn well I've given you plenty of front-handed compliments but you said I was embarrassing you. I'd give you compliments with more than just my hands if you wanted me to. All you have to do is say so, you know how *I* feel.

I know.

Excuse me, I've got to undo my pants...no that's not enough, I guess the zipper has to go too. Ahhh....On Thanksgiving, my sister and I always end up unbuttoning our pants because we eat too much. We lie around afterwards with our pants all the way unzipped and gaping open.

Sounds like you.

Is that some sort of backhanded insult?

No.

This is an awful road—for masochists.

I hate to see you feel this way.

You mean sick?

Yeah, and….

I don't regret it. I'd rather feel this way than go home right now.

But we can turn around. Or we can stop and just sit in the car. Whatever you want, whatever is best for you….

I want to stop and lie down on the road. It looks warm. Hey, you know that demolition derby they had the last night of the fair?

Well, I could hear it. It went till 1 or 2. Screeching tires

Yeah.

and crowd noise and a *Kuntry* band—quite a little lullaby. Sweet dreams, sweetheart.

Oh yeah?

Boy, they loved it. I think they were yelling so loud when the cars crashed, I never heard the sound of crunching metal or popping glass. I'm gonna turn around here. I don't like this road.

Okay, get over to the right and—

I know how to turn a-round. But I'm not going to go back right away. Let's just sit here a while.

Okay.

Does this seat recline? Got any music?

What do you like?

Anything. This feels good. This is real good.

Yes it is.

But we could have lots of good times. Better than this. Better than sitting in a car on the side of the road listening to...what is this, Paul Simon? We

could have better times
than this.

You're scared .

I know.

I guess so.

❖

It just feels so good to
have the sickness fade a-
way out of me. It's like
an aftermath...like after
a fever breaks...every little whisper sounds
beautiful...the slightest
touch of my fingers on
my poor stomach feels
wonderful...I think I can
even smell the sap from
those pine trees. Am I
kinda corny?

Yeah, but I like it.

I could stay here forever,
looking at those thunder-
heads through a tinted
sunroof.

Yeah, but...I hate it that I
have to say stuff like
this...But...

I know. We don't *have* forever. You have to go. You
have to go *back*.

What's that mean?

I'll put it this way: Would
it really be so unusual for
you to invite a pal, a buddy, to that car club event
this weekend?

Probably not....

But you won't invite me.

I guess not.

And where does she think
you are today?

Seeing customers.

And what will you do when
you get back?

Cut the grass. Vacuum the
pool.

Know what I'm gonna do
when I get home?

No.

I don't know either. I'll
decide then. How about
that? I'll decide then. Who
knows what I'll think up.

Well....

Oh fuck it. You wanna
drive again?

❖

I can show you this real neat, fun place on the way back. It's not too far from here. But with you already feeling sick, maybe it's not a good idea.

Maybe I'll just watch you do it. You could let me out and I'll watch you whip past.

Okay. It's right up here. It's a blind uphill high-speed right-hander with an early apex.

It's right here, see, this is the corner. I'll let you out up ahead then go back and do this whole stretch. When I get around this blind corner and pass you, I'll be doing 120 or so. Sure you don't want to feel what it's like?

Whatever that means.

You go ahead.

❖

Move over. I want to drive again.

130

What? Okay. What'd you think—?

It was great. It sounded like a jet engine, a red rocket zooming past. I wanted to be able to see your face up-close while you were doing it. You musta looked really intense.

I guess so....

Didja see that truck pulling in there where you let me off? The driver was having a hard time unlocking the chain across the dirt road. Those three migrants in the back, though, they watched this beautiful, sleek red car go speeding past. But just imagine what they thought when you stopped: a girl gets out and runs across the street while she's zipping up her pants! Then climbs the dirt shoulder, sort of stands there while the car turns around, goes back, and she's still standing there when the car goes by in a red blur with this terrific jet-engine sound, then

131

slows down again, comes around and the girl gets back in.

Oh shit....

What would you have done if they were going the other way...if the truck was pointing toward the road...and if it had pulled out into the road as you came over that blind rise. Could you stop?

Yeah...I'd've stopped all right. But not a pretty sight...God, I'm sorry...I wouldn't've done it if they were pulling out. It would've been stupid. But to tell you the truth, I didn't notice the truck when I let you out. *That* was stupid. What was I thinking?

But you weren't afraid.

I sure would've been if I was aware I was being stupid. But...if I was aware of being stupid, I wouldn't've *been* stupid.

So there's never a reason to be afraid?

I could go for a beer.

A beer is enough.

Yeah, you had the chance of a lifetime...a girl who gets drunk on half a beer.

We could've really gone somewhere. I mean even just today, we could've made it *some*thing today.

My feeling sick isn't what stopped us.

I'm not afraid of any consequences. I'd survive being lost or left. What are you afraid of?

How about just missing something, are you ever afraid you'll pass up a really good thing, that you'll pass up the chance?

We should be afraid of being stupid! God, my heart's pounding too hard now.

I think I need something stiffer than that...all of a sudden....

I remember that....

I know.

I know.

I know.

I don't know.

133

Yes.

I still want to lie down. The road looks like it would be warm, not too hot, perfectly comfortable...like the driveway felt when I used to spend all afternoon in the pool. My mother would yell at us that our lips were blue and it was time to get out, so we would lie on the warm driveway, leaving big wet splotches in the general shapes of bodies. Maybe my lips are blue from the air-conditioner in here. Maybe that's why I'm shivering. Maybe it's time to lie down on the warm pavement and watch the drops falling from my forehead steam when they hit.

That actually sounds... hey, what're you doing?

Turning around.

Why? I've got to—

No, I'll get out and you do the trick again. The blind zooming up-hiller with a right vortex...do it again

134

....I'm not scared—I know how you can handle this thing with perfect ease.

But why? You wanna do it with me this time?

In a way. I'll be waiting right here. Don't worry, I trust you.

BETWEEN SIGNS

Living Legends of the Enchanted Southwest
Watch Authentic Indians,
Handmade crafts, Leather,
Pan for Gold with Real Prospectors

He'll drive with one hand. With the other, unbuttons her shirt. Then when trucks pass, close, going the opposite direction, he'll drive with no hands for a moment, waving to the truckers with his left hand, his right hand never leaving her breasts. She'll arch her back, smile, eyes closed. The wind of the passing trucks will explode against the car like split-second thunderstorms.

Swim
Ski
Relax
Play
In Lostlake City

137

**DO NOT PARK
IN DESIGNATED
PARKING AREAS**

Someday she'll return, using this same road, and it will be late spring, and the migrating desert showers will wash the windshield of collected bugs and dust over and over, and the smell of wet pavement will lift her drooping eyelids, and she'll not stop until she's knocking on his door and it's opening and he's standing there. She'll feel the explosion of his body or the explosion of the door slamming .

**I5 Restaurants
II Motels
Next 2 exits**

RATTLESNAKE-SKIN BOOTS
TURQUOISE BELT BUCKLES
BEADED MOCCASINS, SNO CONES

They took nothing. Credit cards bought gas and food, plastic combs, miniature toothbrushes, motel rooms, tourist T-shirts, foaming shaving cream and disposable razors. She watched him shaving as she lay in the bathtub. Then he shaved her. Rinsing her with the showerhead, soaping her over and over again. Shoved a blob of jelly, from a plastic single-serving container taken from the diner, far inside her, went to retrieve it with his tongue, drop by drop, taste by taste, but there was always more where that came from.

138

See Mystic Magic Of The Southwest...THE THING?

While she takes a turn driving, he'll lay his head in her lap and watch her play with herself. The sound is sticky and sweet like a child sucking candy. The sun will appear and disappear. A band of light across her bare knees. She'll hold his hand and his fingers will join hers moving in and out. The seat wet between her thighs. A cattle crossing will bounce his head in her lap and her legs will tighten around their joined hands. Air coming in the vents is humid, thick with the warm smell of manure, straw, the heat of bodies on the endless flat pasture under the sun. He'll roll to his back to let her wet fingers embrace his erection.

VISIT RUBY FALLS

Make a Bee-Line to ROCK CITY

Don't Miss CATFISH WILLIE'S RIVERBOAT
Restaurant, Lounge, Casino
Fresh Catfish & Hushpuppies
Beulah, Tennessee

Rip Van Winkle Motel just 35 miles

He has no sunglasses. His eyes are slits. Bright white sky and blinking lines on the road. Touches blistered chapped lips with his tongue. Digs into his pocket, sitting on one hip and easing up on the gas. Crackle of paper among the loose change. He unwraps the butterscotch and slips it into his mouth, rolls it with his tongue, coats his mouth with the syrup. When he passes a mailbox on the side of the road, he looks far up the dirt driveway beside it, but can't see where it leads. At the next mailbox, five miles later, he stops for a second. The name on the box says Granger, but, again, the driveway is too long to see what it leads to.

> Triple-Dip ice cream cones
> Camping, ice, propane
> Truckers Welcome

SLIPPERY WHEN WET   FALLING ROCK

They weren't allowed to rent a shower together, so they paid for two but when no one was looking she slipped into his. Someone far away was singing. They stood for a while, back to back, turned and simultaneously leaned against the opposite walls of the shower stall, then slid down and sat facing each other, legs crossing. She told him he looked like he was crying, the water running down his face, but his tears would probably taste soapy. She said once she'd put dish detergent into a doll that was supposed to wet and cry. From then on it had peed foam and bawled suds. He reached out and put a hand on each of her breasts, holding her nipples between two fingers. A door slammed in the stall beside theirs. Water started and a man grunted. He rose to his knees, pulled on her arms so she slid the rest of the way to the floor of the shower, the drain under her back. He eased over her, his mouth moving from breast to breast. Then he lathered her all over, slowly, using almost the whole bar of soap, her ears and neck, toes, ankles, knees, lingering between her legs where the hair was growing back and sometimes itched so badly while they drove that she had to put her hand in her pants and scratch. She was slick to hold. He didn't rinse her before pushing his cock in. The sting of the soap made them open their eyes wide and dig their fingernails into each other's skin. Staring at each other but not smiling.

Taste Cactus Jack's Homestyle Cookin

Relax in Nature's Spa
CHICKEN HOLLER HOT SPRINGS
Sandwiches, Live Bait

ROAD CLOSED IN FLOOD SEASON

Finally she stops and buys half a cantaloupe at a roadside fruit stand. After eating as much as she can with a plastic spoon, she presses her face down into the rind and scrapes the remaining flesh with her teeth. The juice is cool on her cheek and chin. Part of a tattered map, blown by the wind, is propped against the base of a telephone pole. He had laughed at her for getting cantaloupe Marguaritas, but then he'd sipped some of hers, ordered one for himself, said it tasted like her. She breaks the rind in half and slips one piece into her pants, between her legs. The crescent shape fits her perfectly.

MARVEL AT MYTHICAL RELICS
INDIAN JEWELRY
VELVET PAINTINGS

TEXMEX CHICKEN-FRIED STEAK
TACOS, BURRITOS
FREE 72 OZ STEAK IF YOU CAN EAT IT ALL!

When the dirt road gets so bumpy he has to keep both hands on the wheel, she'll take over using the vibrator on herself. He'll watch her, and watch the road. The road always disappears around a bend or beyond a small rise. The car bounces over ruts and rocks. She won't even have to move the vibrator, just hold it inside. She'll say he chose a good road, and her laugh will turn into a long moan, her head thrown over the back of the seat. One of her feet pressed against his leg. Her toes will clutch his pants.

View of Seven States from Rock City

Poison Spring Battleground
next exit, south 12 miles

PIKE COUNTY DIAMOND FIELD
All The Diamonds You Find Are Yours!

For three days he's had a postcard to send home, but can't find the words to explain. It's a picture of the four corners, where Colorado, New Mexico, Arizona and Utah meet. He hadn't gotten down on hands and knees to be in all four states simultaneously. But he had walked around them, one step in each state, making a circle, three times. When he arrives at Chief Yellowhorse's Trading Post and Rock Museum, he buys another postcard, a roadrunner following the dotted

142

line on highway 160. This one's for *her*, wherever she is, if she even left a forwarding address. The rock museum costs a dollar. A square room, glass cases around the edges, dusty brown pebbles with handwritten nametags. Some of the rocks are sawed in half to show blue rings inside. A bin of rose quartz pieces for a nickel each. Black onyx for a dime. Shark's teeth are a quarter.

HOGEYE, pop. 2011
Hogeye Devildogs Football
class D state champs 1971

Behold! Prehistoric Miracles!
Indian Pottery, Sand Paintings
Cochina Dolls, Potted Cactus

Found Alive!
THE THING?

They'll toss their clothes into the back seat. Their skin slippery with sweat. She'll dribble diluted soda over and between his bare legs. Tint of warm root beer smell lingering in the car. She'll hold an ice cube in her lips and touch his shoulder with it. Runs it down his arm. It'll melt in his elbow. She'll fish another ice out of her drink, move it slowly down his chest. When she gets to his stomach, the ice will be gone, her tongue on his skin. She'll keep his hard-on cool by pausing occasionally to slip her last piece of ice into her mouth, then sucking him while he slides a finger in and out of her. The last time she puts the ice into her mouth, his hand will be there to take it from her lips. He'll push the ice

143

into her, roll it around inside with a finger until it's gone. The road lies on the rippling desert like a ribbon. Leaving the peak of each of the road's humps, the car will be airborne for a second.

Cowboy Steaks, Mesquite Broiled

Black Hills Gold, Arrowheads,
Petrified Wood, Chicken Nuggets,
Soda, Thick Milkshakes, Museum
WAGON MOUND TRAVELERS REST

He had to slow down, find a turnout, pull her from the car and half carry her to the shade of a locked utility shack. She dropped to her knees, then stretched out full length on her stomach. He sat beside her, stroking her back. Her body shuddered several more times, then calmed. When she rolled over, the hair on her temples was wet and matted with tears, her eyes thick, murky, glistening, open, looking at him. She smiled.

INDIAN BURIAL MOUNDS NEXT EXIT
GAS, FOOD, LODGING

Rattlesnake Roundup
Payne County Fairgrounds
2nd weekend in July

DUST STORMS NEXT 18 MILES

The waterpark is 48 miles off the main interstate. He's the only car going in this direction and passes no others

144

coming the opposite way. The park was described in a tourbook but wasn't marked on the map. Bumper boats, olympic pool, 3 different corkscrew waterslides, high dive. The only other car in the lot has 2 flat tires. Small boats with cartoon character names painted on the sides are upside down beside an empty concrete pond, a layer of mud and leaves at the bottom. Another layer of dirt at the bottom of the swimming pool is enough to have sprouted grass which is now dry and brown, gone to seed. The scaffold for the waterslides is still standing, but the slides have been dismantled. The pieces are a big aqua-blue pile of fiberglass.

Ancient Desert Mystery . . . THE THING? 157 miles

Land of Enchantment
New Mexico T-Shirts

BULL HORNS
HANDWOVEN BLANKETS
CACTUS CANDY
NATURAL WONDERS

She'll look out the back windshield. The earth is a faint, rolling line against a blue-black sky. His hair tickling her cheek. She'll be on his lap, straddling him, her chin hooked over his shoulder, his cock has been inside her for miles and miles. Sometimes she'll rock slowly from side to side. Sometimes he'll push up from underneath. Sometimes they'll sit and feel the pulse of the engine, the powerful vibration. The air coming through the vent, splashing against her back before it spreads through the car, is almost slightly damp. Smells of rain on pavement, clean and dusty. Out the front windshield, both sky and land stay so dark, there's no line where they meet. No lights and no stars.

If we go west fast enough, will it stay predawn forever?

We can try.

Did you ever pester your parents, When'll we get there, daddy?

And I'd've thought it was torture if he said *never*.

GOSPEL HARMONY HOUSE CHRISTIAN DINNER THEATRE

MERGING TRAFFIC   DEER XING   SHARP CURVES
                                                                      NEXT 10 MILES

They started walking toward the entrance of the WalMart store, but she turned off abruptly, crossed a road and climbed a small hill where someone had set up three crosses in the grass. They were plant stakes lashed together. Kite string was tangled on a tumbleweed. When she got back to the parking lot, five or six big cockleburs were clinging to each of her socks. She sat on the hood of the car picking them off. When he came from the store with two blankets, toilet paper, aspirin and glass cleaner, she said, There weren't any graves up there after all. He put the bag in the back seat, turned and smiled. Kiss me, she said.

Meteor Crater and gift shop, 3 miles ➡

WARNING:
THIS ROAD CROSSES A U.S.
AIR FORCE BOMBING RANGE
FOR THE NEXT 12 MILES DANGEROUS
OBJECTS MAY DROP FROM AIRCRAFT

BIMBO'S FIREWORKS
Open all year

He spreads a map over his steering wheel. This road came forty-five miles off the interstate. He pays and follows the roped-off trail, stands looking at the cliff dwellings as the guide explains which was the steam room, which compartment stored food, which housed secret rituals, where the women were allowed to go and where they weren't, why they died off before white settlers ever arrived, and the impossibly straight narrow paths which connected them directly to other cliff dwelling cities and even now were still visible from the sky, spokes on a wheel converging on their religious center.

Bucksnort Trout Pond
Catch a Rainbow!

Krosseyed Kricket Kampground

Two Guns United Methodist Church
Sunday Worship 10 a.m.
Visitors Welcome

She doesn't even know how long she's been sitting by

the side of the road. The car shakes when the semis go past. Sometimes she can see a face turned toward her for a split second. The last time she went behind a rock to pee, she found three big black feathers with white tips. Now she's holding one, brushing it lightly over her face. Her eyes are closed. Somehow the scent of the feather is faintly wild. When she returns—in a year, two years, five years—in heavy sleep long past midnight but long before dawn, he'll never know any time passed at all. Like so many nights before she left, her footsteps will pad down the sidewalk. The nurse who shares his life will long since have put on her white legs and horned hat and gone to the hospital. Using the key he made for her, which she still carries on her chain, she'll let herself in. Move past the odor of hairspray in the bathroom. Drop her clothes in a heap in the doorway— simple clothes she'll easily be able to pull on in the moments before she leaves him. Then she'll stand there, listen to his body resting. Watch the dim form of him under the sheet become clearer. She'll crawl to the bedside, lean her elbows and chin on the mattress, his hand lying open near her face. She'll touch his palm with the wild feather, watch the fingers contract and relax. Until his hand reaches for her, pulls her into the bed and remembers her. She opens her eyes and squints although dusk has deadened the glare on the road. Slips the feather behind one ear. She doesn't remember which direction she'd been going before she stopped here to rest.

BRIDGE FREEZES IN COLD WEATHER

148

The Unknown is Waiting For You!
See The Thing? just 36 more miles

STATE PRISON
Do Not Stop For Hitchhikers

Yield

The music channel hadn't had any music for a while. She sat up, stared at the screen, counted the number of times either the interviewer or musician said *man*, lost track quickly, changed to the weather station, turned the sound down. She massaged his shoulders and back, each vertebra, his butt, his legs, the soles of his feet, each toe. He said, I'm yours forever. Said it into the pillow. Anything you want, he said. She lay her cheek against his back and watched a monsoon, palm trees bending to touch the tops of cottages, beach furniture thrown through windows. He had rolled over and was looking at her. His eyes looked almost swollen shut. Anything, he said. She looked back at the screen, yachts tossed like toys, roofs blown off, an entire pier folded sideways along the beach. She said, I've never been in something like that.

He pinned her wrists in just one of his hands, hurled her face-down. She was open and ready as though panting heavy fogged air from her cunt, and he slammed himself in there, withdrew completely and slammed in again and again. With each thrust she said, Oh! And he answered when he came, a long, guttural cry, releasing her wrists to hold onto her hips and pump her body on his cock.

149

They lay separate for a while. Now, she said, hold me...with both hands. Hold me like something you'd never want to break. Tomorrow I'll drop you off at the nearest airport.

SPECIAL PERMIT REQUIRED FOR:
Pedestrians
Bicycles
Motor Scooters
Farm Implements
Animals on Foot

Home of Johnny Johnson
Little All-American 1981

Ice Cream, Divinity, Gas, Picnic Supplies
Real Indians Performing Ancient Rites

He'll set the car on cruise control and they'll each climb out a window, pull themselves to the roof of the car, to the luggage rack. Their hair and clothes lash and snap in the rushing wind. Dawn has been coming on for hours. The sun may never appear. The sky behind them pink-gold on the horizon, bleeding to greenish, but like wet blue ink straight above them. She'll unbutton her shirt and hold her arms straight up, lets the wind undress her. They'll take turns loosening their clothes and feeling thin, cool rushing air whip the material away. Bursting through low pockets of fog, they come out wet and sparkling, tingling, goosebumped. They'll slide their bodies together, without hurry and without holding back, no rush to get anywhere, saving nothing for later, passing the same rocks, bushes and fenceposts over and over. As the car leaves the road, leaping and bounding with naive zest, they'll pull each other closer and hold on, seeing the lovely sky in each other's eyes, tasting the sage and salty sand on each other's skin, hearing the surge of velocity in the other's shouted or breathless laughter, feeling the tug of joy in their guts, in their vigorous appetites. The sky still deep violet-black, the dawn still waiting, the car still soaring from butte to pinnacle to always higher peaks.

INTRODUCING THE BLACK ICE BOOKS SERIES:

The Black Ice Books Series will introduce readers to the new generation of dissident writers in revolt. Breaking out of the age-old traditions of mainstream literature, the voices published here are at once ribald, caustic, controversial, and inspirational. These books signal a reflowering of the art underground. They explore iconoclastic styles that celebrate life vis-à-vis the spirit of their unrelenting energy and anger. Similar to the recent explosion in the alternative music scene, these books point toward a new counterculture rage that's just now finding its way into the mainstream discourse. The Black Ice Books Series brings to readers the most radical fiction being written in America today.

The Kafka Chronicles
A novel by Mark Amerika
The Kafka Chronicles investigates the world of passionate sexual experience while simultaneously ridiculing everything that is false and primitive in our contemporary political discourse. It accomplishes this dual task by following the activities of a cast of angry yet sensual characters. Meet Alkaloid Boy and Blue Sky, an inconspicuous and loving couple who find themselves subjected to constant government harassment; General Psyche and his sidekick Major Uptight, the military officers responsible for controlling the media briefing room during the Gulf War; King Bohemia, the guerrilla-artist who hosts wild orgies; and, of course, Gregor Samsa, who wakes up one day and finds himself an explosive living in the eco-anarchy of postmodern America. Mark Amerika's first novel ignites hyper-language that explores the relationship between style and substance, self and sexuality, and identity and difference. His energetic prose uses all

available tracks, mixes vocabularies, and samples genres. Taking its cue from the recent explosion of angst-driven rage found in the alternative rock music scene, this book reveals the unsettled voice of America's next generation.

Mark Amerika has lived in Florida, New York, California, and different parts of Europe, and has worked as a free-lance bicycle courier, lifeguard, video cameraman, and greyhound racing official. His fiction has been compared to that of Mark Leyner. Amerika's fiction has appeared in many magazines, including *Fiction International*, *Witness*, the German publication *Lettre International*, and *Black Ice*, of which he is editor. He is presently writing a "violent concerto for deconstructive guitar" in Boulder, Colorado.

"Mark Amerika not only plays music—the rhythm, the sound of his words and sentences—he plays verbal meanings as if they're music. I'm not just talking about music. Amerika is showing us that William Burroughs came out of jazz knowledge and that now everything's political—and everything's coming out through the lens of sexuality..."
—*Kathy Acker*

Paper, ISBN: 0-932511-54-6, $7.00

Revelation Countdown
Short Fiction by Cris Mazza
While in many ways reaffirming the mythic dimension of being on the road already romaticized in American pop and folk culture, *Revelation Countdown* also subtly undermines that view. These stories project onto the open road not the nirvana of personal freedom but rather a type of freedom more closely resembling loss of control. Being in constant motion and passing through new environments destabilizes life, casts it out of phase, heightens perception, skews reactions. Every little problem is magnified to overwhelming dimensions; events segue from slow motion to fast forward;

background noises intrude, causing perpetual wee-hour insomnia. Imagination flourishes, often as an enemy: people suddenly discover that they never really understood their traveling companions. The formerly stable line of their lives veers off course. In such an atmosphere, the title *Revelation Countdown*, borrowed from a roadside sign in Tennessee, proves prophetic: It may not arrive at 7:30, but revelation will inevitably find the traveler.

"...fictions that are remarkable for the force and freedom of their imaginative style."
—*New York Times Book Review*

"Talent jumps off her like an overcharge of electricity."
—*Los Angeles Times*

Cris Mazza is the author of two previous collections of short fiction, *Animal Acts* and *Is It Sexual Harassment Yet?* and a novel, *How to Leave a Country*. She has resided in Brooklyn, New York; Clarksville, Tennessee; and Meadville, Pennsylvania; but she has always lived in San Diego, California.

Paper, ISBN: 0-932511-73-2, $7.00

Avant-Pop: Fiction for a Daydream Nation
Edited by Larry McCaffery
In *Avant-Pop*, Larry McCaffery has assembled a collection of innovative fiction, comic book art, illustrations, and other unclassifiable texts written by the most radical, subversive, literary talents of the postmodern new wave. The authors included here vary in background, from those with well-established reputations as cult figures in the pop underground (Samuel R. Delany, Kathy Acker, Ferret, Derek Pell, Harold Jaffe), and important new figures who have gained prominence since the late eighties (Mark Leyner, Eurudice, William T. Vollmann), to, finally, the most promising new kids on the block, such as "rap fiction" master Ricardo Cortez

Cruz and Doug Rice, whose obscenely obsessive, Faulkner-meets-Acker prose is showcased here for the first time.

Avant-Pop is meant to send a collective wake-up call to all those readers who spent the last decade nodding off, along with the rest of America's daydream nation. To those readers and critics who have decried the absence of genuinely radicalized art capable of liberating people from the bland roles and assumptions they've accepted in our B-movie society of the spectacle, Avant-Pop announces that reports about the death of a literary avant-garde have been greatly exaggerated.

Larry McCaffery's most recent books include Storming the Reality Studio: A Casebook of Cyberpunk and Postmodern SF and Across the Wounded Galaxies: Interviews with Contemporary American SF Writers.

Paper, ISBN: 0-932511-72-4, $7.00

New Noir
Stories by John Shirley

In New Noir, John Shirley, like a postmodern Edgar Allen Poe, depicts minds deformed into fantastic configurations by the pressure, the very weight, of an entire society bearing down on them. "Jody and Annie on TV," selected by the editor of Mystery Scene as "perhaps the most important story…in years in the crime fiction genre," reflects the fact that whole segments of zeitgeist and personal psychology have been supplanted by the mass media, that the average kid on the streets in Los Angeles is in a radical crisis of exploded self-image, and that life really is meaningless for millions. In "I Want to Get Married, Says the World's Smallest Man," a crack prostitute's state of mind degenerates so far as to become entirely mechanical. "War and Peace" shows cops being cops the way cops are really cops. The stories here also bring to mind Elmore Leonard and the better crime novel-ists, but John Shirley—unlike writers who attempt to ex-